F IC   Healy, Dermot.

        Banished misfortune,
        and other stories

BANISHED MISFORTUNE

Dermot Healy was born in Finea, County Westmeath, Ireland, in 1947. He has lived in Cavan and Dublin, and now lives in London. He has two children. He has published poetry and prose in many magazines and anthologies, has received two Hennessy Literary Awards (1974, 1976), and has written, directed and acted in a number of films and plays. In 1980 he was the winning director in the All-Ireland Drama Festival with his production of *Waiting for Godot* and most recently wrote the screenplay for the film *Our Boys*, directed by Cathal Black. He is also the editor of *The Drumlin*, a Cavan-based literary-local-historical magazine. *Banished Misfortune* is his first collection of stories, and *Fighting with Shadows*, his first novel, will be published in the autumn of 1982.

Banished Misfortune

and other stories

by

Dermot Healy

ALLISON & BUSBY/LONDON • NEW YORK
BRANDON/IRELAND

FIC

First published in Great Britain 1982
by Allison & Busby Limited,
6a Noel Street, London W1V 3RB
and distributed in the USA
by Schocken Books Inc.
200 Madison Avenue, New York, NY 10016.

First published in Ireland
by Brandon Book Publishers Limited,
Dingle, Co. Kerry.

British Library Cataloguing in Publication Data

Healy, Dermot
  Banished misfortune, and other stories
  I. Title
  823'.914 [F] PR6058.E
Allison & Busby: ISBN 0-85031-456-9
Brandon: ISBN 0-86322-003-7

The author wishes to thank the Irish Arts Council for
their bursary in 1978.

The publishers wish to acknowledge the financial
assistance of the Arts Council of Great Britain.

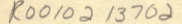

R00102 13702

Typeset 10/11 Plantin
by Alan Sutton Publishing Limited, Gloucester.
Printed and bound in Great Britain by
Richard Clay, (The Chaucer Press) Limited, Bungay, Suffolk

Contents

Acknowledgements are due to the following publications where some of these stories first appeared:

Irish Press, Dublin, 1974 and *Firebird I*, ed. T.J. Binding, Penguin Books, Harmondsworth, 1982 ("First Snow of the Year"); *Irish Press*, Dublin, 1975, and *Best Irish Short Stories* ed. David Marcus, Elek Books, London, 1976 ("Banished Misfortune"); *Icarus* ed. Eddie Brazill, Trinity College Dublin magazine, 1975 ("The Girl in the Muslin Dress"); *Cyphers*, Dublin, 1977 and *Paddy No More*, Longship Press, Nantucket, 1977 ("The Island and the Calves"); *A Soft Day* ed. Sean Golden and Peter Fallon, University of Notre Dame Press, Indiana, 1980 ("A Family and a Future"); *Images*, Dublin, 1980 ("Reprieve").

for
Winnie, Anne and Maura

First Snow of the Year

FOR A FEW bewildering seconds, Jim Philips, on the day of his retirement, queried late morning sounds he had not heard in years. Then his solitary sense of freedom began. He looked with leisure at the low pink boards that ran the length of the ceiling, yellowing at the fireplace, brightening by the window.

Light was hammering on the broken shutter.

Shadows darted across the mildewed embroidery of dogs and flowers.

He cleared his womanless bed with a light heart, glad to have outgrown the ache in his smothered loins, outlived his job that he might die in a time of his own making. He nimbly laid his drinking clothes before last night's fire, coaxed first with paraffin, then whiskey. He hung his postman's uniform in the closet under the stairs.

He buttoned himself up for the air.

The ground was rock-hard and early frost had frozen the colours about the bog. The valley across which he had been a messenger for thirty years lay stretched out below him in a state of moral predictability. He saw John and Margaret Cawley, the gypsies, stealing through the yellow gorse with rotten turf. Their children moved from clownish tree to clownish tree out of the wind.

He shattered the surface water of the well, and from where Jim stood, the earth was on its side, reflected in every piece of ice, the wind sounding through the gulleys and drains like a concert flute. The bitter cold cleared his scalp and breath as he walked back. Young Phildy was standing under the gable. He felt a kind of fatalism seeing Phildy there, out of the wind looking at the earth, humourless and uncertain. Phildy threw in some frost-flecked sods of turf for the old man and then waited about impatiently till they were ready to go down.

Phildy stood under the gable again, surly-looking, but of sudden times, nearly by inspiration, his tall frame would relax, his face ruffle with silent laughter.

The bell sounded.

"What are you thinking about?" asked Jim.

"Nothing. There's no change."

"We'll look down from the hill."

Phildy did not answer, but mumbled, with a hint of anger was it, in his voice.

They came to the edge of a small mossy clearing and looked toward the funeral. Jim dropped to his knee. The children of Liz's relations tottered among the appealing shapes of stone and foreign marble, flowers under glass, and when the priest stooped to say the final prayers the mourners turned left and studied Stagg's grave, the hunger-striker who had died in England. Owen Beirne, the son of the dead woman, and his jovial uncles delivered Liz on their shoulders and light as mercury she was lowered down cautiously with leather straps.

The long-jawed undertaker paid out the clay with jerky fingers into the son's palm.

Snow began amid the hand-shaking.

Helen stood with Phildy's child away from the mourners like a stranger. Owen Beirne's woman now, she once was Phildy's. Phildy moved toward her as Jim Philips joined the throng by the grave. Phildy said to himself, "Not to be possessed, not that." Phildy said to himself, "I have no desire ever to lie in her bed again." Helen looked closely at him, the child leaped into his arms. They swung round and round, and when they stopped Phildy said to her, "If you have a baby by that bastard, I'll come and cut it out of your stomach."

The dreadful shapes of the parish surrounded them with guilt and terror. She turned her head.

Phildy moved off with Jim by the History Road, through land killed over, by the Four Altars of stone, past the secluded oak trees that shelter the unfrightened children who died before Christ, a flowerless limbo for the unbaptized in the corner of a field, over the bridge where REMEMBER STAGG was written in coarse white lettering, past the American cars and the hikers sitting smoking in a ditch.

"What did he say?" asked Owen, taking Helen by the hand and then the elbow.

"He said he would kill me," she replied.

"Wait at the house for me," he said.

Phildy and Jim walked into the dim light of O'Grady's public house. "I have been considering what you might call a new theory," said Devine, the second-hand-watch man, his shiny waist-coat and nose covered with snuff, "I have read recently that turf, mind you, if properly compressed could provide a queer cheap and powerful source of power. And I mean well beyond the briquette stage."

"This round is on me," said O'Grady without enthusiasm. In honour of Jim Philips, postman, recently retired. O'Grady set up an electric kettle on a stout crate and dropped a measure of cloves and sugar into each glass. His wife was throwing darts with the boys in the bar. The light was right for drinking by. Elephants from a circus roared from a nearby town. The radio said: "Walton's, your weekly reminder of the grace and beauties that lie —"

"I'll have a woman above in the house in no time, true as God," spoke Jim.

"Smell that," said Phildy.

Phildy went into the lounge and took a cue off some of the young lads playing there. He missed an easy ball. He broke up the pool game for no good reason. He turned one of the young fellow's arms behind his back. He pulled him to him. "What were you saying?" he asked. The young fellow looked him in the eye. Phildy left two shillings on the table.

He strolled back to the men.

"— when that fellow was a child," continued Jim, "along with his brother I used to push them happily along in a tub down a sheugh off the mountain, and every time I was ready to quit, your man there, Phildy, would pipe up: 'Ah, just once more'. Back up again and start all over. Well, I pushed till night fell and now they've grown and taken all my demesne and I wouldn't say a word against their father."

Their thoughts faded into the interior.

In a field over from there a circle gambling formed around a penny or a bird, a cock crowed by the wheel of a wagon, the sixth bird lost an eye and a wing was slung in a ditch, and the handler picked blood and feathers out of the mouth of the seventh and breathed life back into him, sucked at his beak and rubbed his chin murmuring along the back of the fighter, while the trainer stood away from the fight, another tossing bag in his hand ready with the oiling tape, the washer and the weights. The men stood with the weight of their feet on their money.

"I saw them go by this morning," O'Grady whispered.

"Did you now," said Jim.

"I did. Dowds did the burying."

"Was it now."

"Dowds it was."

"Driving like a ginnet he was."

"Is that a fact."

"That'll do," said Devine.

Owen Beirne watched the sparse mourners leave through the falling snow. It must have been years since any of them had laid eyes on her, yet the old came here faithfully from their rooms in a vast acreage of wind and cold. Uncle James sneezed and sneezed. Helen, who had nursed his mother up to the day she died, had left dispiritedly, as if she had never once visited misfortune, nor taken old men dispassionately out of their rheumy beds to insert a catheter. Holding their shoddy under-garments. Weeding them of fading hair from armpit and groin. She was terrified for her child and herself. Of other minds speaking with her eyes, her tongue.

His mourning uncles talked of going up the village.

Their families had gone ahead in near ecstasy.

"A man can best fix the orifices of the world," said Devine.

"Helen pressed with her thumbs to see the cat's eye of death," whispered the barman, "powdered and combed Liz to a child."

"Jesus Christ, stop the sound of that man's voice," raised Phildy.

"Your the beast of the mirage, boy," advised Jim.

"Now Phildy, take it easy," said O'Grady.

"Will you stop talking," cried Phildy. His intestines shivered and grew weighty. He saw Owen withdraw from Helen, coursing his penis through her hands. His blood no longer went freely between the isolated and unbalanced part of himself. His white Christian bones grew rigid.

"As bas as 'forty-seven," said Jim when after the first skirmish the void began, and the door opened into the pub to admit Mr O'Dowd, undertaker, grocery-cum-pub owner. He kicked back with his boots as he surveyed the company. Jerky movements fretted around his temple and fingers.

"The worst," he said.

"— ah, but not interrupting you there," said the watch-man, as he looked into the distance, studs rattling, "but that 'forty-seven blizzard wasn't so bad in the morning, but by evening it could smother a body. For I lay in my bed that night without an ounce of sleep, thinking myself grown to a statue, and the following morning I lay on and on thinking it was dark, and get up I did, eventually, pushed open the door after a long harangue and lo and behold you, it was bright. . . ."

"There is no mystery to the whore," said Phildy.

Owen Beirne sat in an empty pub at the back of a grocery among the tinned beans, Chef bottles of sauce, Saxo packets of salt, where every time someone entered to do their shopping a crisp otherworld bell rang. The soft smell of flour and more bitter odour of rotting vegetables hung in the air. A rich woman delayed over the trade names of certain goods till he hated the living sight of her. A child with his mother's face smiled at him from the woman's pram. The smell of the flour seemed to come from his own living flesh. In that acute silence which the spirit of the dead make their own. And at last his mourning uncles arrived and they talked and talked, the first drink was for sorrow and the second for joy. Owen carried Uncle Festy, a disturbing old villain, to his Ford van. An explosion in a nearby river rocked the street. The other relations left, speaking with great understanding and humour. His uncles' empty glasses filled the wooden counter. There was nowhere on that counter he could rest his hand with the fingers spread, nor know what should be darkened and what brightened. Thinking of Helen was the last cheerful thing in the world.

"Man to man," Uncle Festy said as he lowered him into the driver's seat. The children were singing in the back. "Remember Frank Stagg," said he. And lastly, "Take your own road, no matter what," said he and his eyes watering.

"And I opened the door and looked out and, lo and behold you, it was bright," the watch-man Devine continued, "so bright that it

5

would dazzle your eyes . . . and I stood at the door and I called, and I went up the low hill from the door and I called and called . . . the sister within shouting at the greyhound like a woman tormented . . . and I thought all my beasts were dead, taken from me during the night . . . when, Lord save me, out of the drifts by the galvanize shed they came, one by one, struggling up toward me like the newborn . . . and I fed them like a man whose wits had got the better of him . . . nudging and poking at my chest . . . Lord, wasn't I the happy man when they came up striking out of the snow and took the hay without a word."

"For one bright sovereign sold my life away," a cockfighter was singing. Trucks lumbered into the council yard across the valley. The roads were quick as lightning.

The great juggernauts moved out of the milk factory and turned their dipped lights onto the white plains. Mrs O'Grady, the publican's wife, looked like she might live forever.

"'Throw the clay on top of me,' wailed the sergeant, climbing on top of his dead wife's coffin, and then he turned round and married another."

Stones were hurled across the polythene to keep the peat dry.

And the sea drove shells into the cairn, sounding in Owen's ears as he rode a stolen bike crazily down the hill from the village, swerving in the torrents of snow. The white of the road curved into a single turning tyre. The colours on every side gathered into a frenzied shape, time slowed down to the independent moment. Helen, so delicate a thing, trussed up in the snow beside the grave. The begging trees on the mountain crisp as a child's brain. Owen feared the men looking for him. Those that tormented Helen. And that moment he heard the chisels at work undoing the image of his mother, he flew up the rafters to see. First they shaped those perfect eyes, then gouged them out. Circled and released the breasts with care, and when he looked back they were gone. The cheeks. The back of the head. The builder held his cheek to the small lift of the stomach. Then suddenly butted his head into the interior and the whole figure gave way. When he looked back, the builder was gone. Owen freewheeled on till, at Edmonstown Cross, he went into a ditch with awkward attempts to save himself. As the wheels hit the grass margin deep down, he was carried round and round on his back a few yards up the road.

Phildy, on his way back from O'Grady's, had seen the final impact. He stood silently watching from the far side of the road where everything was normal, not moving, blindfolded. With him stood two other young witnesses, dressed in great gaberdines and boots, their hair pommaded beneath woollen caps. A snowdrift in a sheugh had nearly covered Owen, he surrendered gladly to the shock of the fall, lay quiet, swallowed blood from a cut on his lip. He gathered the feeling of pain back into his bones. He raised himself onto his elbows, moaning, onto his knees and stayed there a while till gradually he focused on the dark figures silhouetted against the snow-tipped, serrated evergreens. As he watched, a figure would appear and disappear, stepping forward, stepping backward. Owen called across. "Let it be now, just yourself and myself." The man standing kicked him on the bottom of the spine. "That's for Helen," Phildy said. The others hammered into his face with the violent devotion of the obsessed. Then Phildy pulled the others off Owen and they went up toward Monestrevin, their anger anaesthetized by nature for a time. "Come back and fight, you cunts!" Owen shouted after the retreating ghosts. He gathered himself and roared helplessly. "One at a time," he shouted after them.

"And a few days later," Devine went on, "I took the gun and went down to Lough Gara and I shot some wild ducks, the urchin that I was, 'cause there wasn't a bit of food in the house . . . not a bit. . . . Sure there was no eating in them . . . and that mad creature of a spaniel I had rose the poor things, and up they got fighting their cause."

"Yes," said Jim Philips, "and the trams, what with the drifts of 'forty-seven, stopped that day in Brighton."

The undertaker hammered his heels and buttoned his coat up tightly about him. "Two hot whiskeys for the gentlemen," he asked, "and a small brandy for myself."

Owen's feet dragged through the silence like many people walking. While the studs of the watch-man's boots clinked in the yard, and the postman thought of the turf above, it was to fall into Helen's arms Owen desired. He ran this way and that, terrified of the long drop into the bogholes, his senses failed him, he could make nothing of this white silence where the particles of the mind were dispersed so quietly. He had never known this blind panic before. He stood for a long time trying to get his bearings, but the light was the same everywhere, not the separate light toward which the individual can turn, shining in his own beauty, but dispersed so freely that a great weary record of endless detail began.

"I would not want to be struggling with a woman as to my worth. Not that thing."

"Nor be a woman, mending my ways for others, that little pleasure come of it."

"A new frustration cannot enter the world," said the undertaker resignedly.

"The kali."

"The auld culcannon."

"A skillet full of kali, with the onions and the homemade butter."

"That's the stuff."

"And the boxty."

"The boxty. Ah, man dear."

"And the potato cake."

"Stop! Stop!"

It stopped snowing, the brittle stars came out. Would the dead forgive him if his hands had wandered over Helen's face in the darkness of the mourning house, touching and parting flesh here, and folding his body around her against death. The canoe to the sea. He walked across a new planet, journeying inwards, without thought of his fellows. There were so many clear stars that he found the gravel track on the far side of the bog as in a dream, all beaten up and restored, like the others of his tribe. He ran forward through the shells of snow-filled houses where the elders had lived it all. Through deserted kitchens, middens, bedrooms with nothing to be seen, hearths filled with torn fishing-nets, old potato gardens drilled hard with the frost, turf stiff with snow. He came to Phildy's house, plastered with gravel and ivy, the laughter of the men echoed back from the trees. Sparks flew from the chimney. The abandoned pram on the path filled with berries. He came to his own house. There was no one there. Owen did not search long but followed the horses' path up to the rocks. He crossed the rocks. The stars so low he could have blown them out.

First Snow of the Year

Helen was sitting in the gypsy tent babysitting, looking after little Barney and Roger. Her own child asleep between them. The parents were over the road drinking. "Sh," she said. He came in and sat beside her. They sat in utter silence. When the children woke, she spoke in gypsy talk to reassure them. He filled the stove with timber and turf, snow dripped from the black canvas. He laid his head on her shoulder and they kissed in a direct trusting manner. Soon John Cawley and Margaret Cawley came over the rocks singing dead verse.

A Family and a Future

I NEVER SAW them go out that way in their cars by night. The new Ford Consuls, perhaps a Morris Minor. Volkswagens were always popular round that recalcitrant time. I can only imagine the secrets the night holds, the vulnerability of the isolated sex-object, the daring curiosity of those frightened, frustrated men and always the rumours of decadent tragedy. Perhaps those frightened, sharp-suited men would be walking up the road throwing nervous glances to the left and right of them. Or more assuredly, I'd say, in the heat of drink and summer they would drive bravely out to that beautiful place, where the Erne breaks sparklingly asunder between the forests, play the horn going past the cottage and collect her at her innocent, prearranged places.

For this is real pornography, to imagine the habits of June rather than describe them with authenticity, those quick flitting affairs where Sheelin thundered. Or the beat of visionary passion across an ancient cemetery overrun with shadows, for illicit lovers have always favoured as their first jousting place the quiet of the grave.

June was three years older than myself. She lived with an ailing though resilient mother, cantankerous, shoddy, quick-witted from dealing aggressively with shy people and successful farmers. June's father had been carried off by a fever from drinking contaminated water. Thus she took on the feeding of the few cattle that remained, carrying buckets of water from a spring well a mile away, dousing her socks, since the nearby well had never been cleared up or lime-stoned after the poisoning. She looked after the chopping of timber from the multitudinous forest of the Lord, facilitated dispassionately and excitedly the emissions of her neighbourly brethren.

From the locality she extended her doings to the town.

What had been mere sensual caprice became decadent business overnight.

I never then saw her in a pub or encountered her on the way to the Cathedral.

Befitting a hard worker, her body was strong but fat. She was not in the least goodlooking. But, because of the dark lashes, June's brown eyes confirmed that traditional estimation of beauty by the Gaelic bards of the area. . . . You, the highest nut in the place. Tanned from wandering the fields after lost cattle she would wander through the market on fair day, watched by the treacherous eyes of the stall-holders, in ribbons and patched skirt, huge hips akimbo. The Louis heels of her pink shoes worn sideways because of the edge of her walk, dots of mud on the back of her seamed nylons. The street-corner folk would hail her as she passed. She might loiter by the winter Amusements, a little astray among the jargon of lights and fortune-telling, in those days when the giddy voice of Buddy Holly filled the side-streets with "I guess it doesn't matter any more". But she was always attracted to the rifle range. Cold-blooded curses helped her aim. Her brown eyes squinted down and steadied on the centre of life, on the yellow thin heart of a crow, on the marked cap of a jester.

I was never attracted to her but we always spoke. Like Hallo, and How is the crack, and How is it going.

But I did see her father's polka-dotted tie that held up her worn knickers.

I was sick, about thirteen and on the back of a bike travelling along the edge of the railway lines. Sweeney dropped the bike when he saw June chasing a Red Devon cow across a field, from east to west, and the two of them fell together among the coltsfoot and daffodils, stripped in the frost and she masturbated him and then me, and there was something virulent about his satisfaction, something slow and remorselessly painful about mine.

It was her desire and detachment, my desire of love. And then Sweeney mounted her some time later and she called to him, for a minute Stop, stop, you're hurting, but he didn't and then she fainted. Her brown face keeled over in the frost, her father's tie round her ankles, and a look of horrified petulance on his face, he stood under a leafless oak, his brown cock unbloodied but fading. He would I think have buried her there had she not come to. But what did I say or do in those moments? Nursed her head in my lap, called to her, sung to her? Was I not at that moment as much to blame for her misfortune? But Sweeney returned with water and

11

aspirins from a nearby house, she drank as I coaxed her, her eyes swam and steadied and then she thanked us, once more restored, she set off to capture the beast she had been following. And Sweeney shouted after her, I'm sorry June, and many's the time after they were lovers. For years too I was afflicted by this scene, in my dream I would, too, be about to come, and try to restrain for fear of hurting her, wake painfully in the dark, sperm like acid on my thighs. No, she never went into a pub for she never reached the peak of adult debauchery. Hers will always be the brink, the joyous, disparate moments of adolescence. Till none of the country folk bothered her, till she became the shag, the ride, the jaunt of the town. Eventually the police took a hand and barred her from the precincts, from her nocturnal clambering into parked buses at the depot, doors opened by skilled mechanics, from stretching under an impatient, married man in the waiting-room of the railway station. Thus those cars would be leaving town to pick up June, single or in groups, in the hubbub of careless laughter to spread her juices across the warm leather upholstery.

It was around this time that Benny met her, I think. He had been hired out to a farm in Dundalk for five years previous, and one full lush May he returned for the cancerous death of his last parent. Benny had a red freckled face, wore hunting caps, was a loner. He took her to the pictures, her first normal romance began. She was under great distress, as it was her first time in the cinema and they moved twice till she was immaculately placed one row behind the four-pennies. It was not short-sightedness but enthusiasm. Over his shoulder she stole timorous, enquiring glances at Maureen O'Hara, as the square filled up with wounded soldiers from the Civil War. Benny was to linger on a further three years in Dundalk, but that December he returned again to his deserted house, they cut trees together in the Christmas tree wood and sold them in the snowed-up market place, two shillings apiece, a week before the festival. Pheasants were taken with a shot of blood and feathers from the cloudy skies above Sheelin and presented by him to June's house for the seasonal dinner. Which he attended, the wily gossiping stranger, with a bottle of Jameson and orange.

But that was the first Christmas. The second or third he never came. June had mothered a child. By a solicitor, a priest, by myself, does it matter? That summer too her mother made it to the bath in time to vomit up a three-foot tapeworm. The old lady's skin and bone retreated under the shock. The release of the worm and birth of the child occurred within a week of each other. June grew thin again, her mother fattened. They grew more friendly, dependent upon each other. That year too, during these trying times, when they were burning the gorse and the furze, a fire swept the hill behind the house. And the two sick ladies fought the flames, shouting encouragement to each other, retreated successfully, covered in ash, their blouses scorched, their arms thrown around each other, laughing, and stood together that evening holding up the newly washed child to look at the smoking field.

Neighbours came and mended their own fences and kept their counsel to themselves.

The drama of that fiery evening was that it led to a reunion between Benny and June and the dry-skinned baby. He came and repaired the scorched sheds, replaced the burnt rafter, renailed the twisted galvanize and played with the child in the cool kitchen, braved the mad, wandering talk of the mother. From the window you could see the water breaking out there like it was hitting water-coloured rocks. Sails skimmed through the trees, boat engines roared, and behind, a less formidable beauty, endowed darkly and modern among the pines, with wooden seats and toilets for viewing the lake, a black modern café with chain motifs on a cleared rise.

Soon the tourists would be arriving. "To paint a dark corner darker," the old lady said. "Think of who sired him that built yon." She held the bowl of soup at arm's length, licking her wrists and fists, grey brown-tinged hair, deep-blue flowered nightcoat, fluffy shoes, yellow nightdress peeking out at her strained neck, awkward movements. "The architect, the gobshite, came in here to explain, all airs and graces. Then he started a fucking dirge. We told him where to get off."

June was on the grass, on all fours, scrambling away from the child and Benny smoked by the window.

They married, herself and Benny, the following April. And the next time I saw them was at a dance at the opening of that café, where as yet only light drinks were being served, given by the local

13

GAA. I was mesmerized after a day's drinking, and in drunken fashion attended to their every need, needing heroes myself, but at some point I got into an argument and was set upon by a couple of bastards from the town. They ripped at my face with fingers like spurs, broken glass tore at my throat. I heard the band breaking down, heels grated against my teeth. Lying there babbling and crying on the floor while the fight went on over my head. June came and hauled me free and Benny swung out left, right and centre. They caught Benny's eye a fearful blow and all I can remember is an Indian doctor in the hospital complaining of having had enough of attending to drunks in the middle of the night. But a nurse stitched my scalp back onto my head and my head back onto my body.

As for Benny, he was taken away to the Eye and Ear Hospital in Dublin where he was ably attended to and where I called on him. We shared few words, because only fighting brought out the intimacy in us. My life then for a number of years was spent in aggravating silly details. Benny returned to Dundalk to complete a final year and June took on other lovers, she mothered another child. With his money saved Benny returned a year later in spring for good. Shrunken reeds had washed up, carquet, light brown, two ducks flying together, the dark blowing in. Cars were parked on the entrance to the café, which was now a magnificent hotel, with C & W stickers on them. The little Pleasure House of the Lord of the Estate had been renewed by the Minister of Lands with new bright pebble-dash, and renamed. Going up a new lane seemed miles, coming back mere yards.

I was out at the Point after an endless day's fishing without a catch, curlews screaming in the background, cormorants fanning themselves in heraldic postures at the top of the castle. Benny and I stood together chatting. But aloof, too, from each other, for things change; sometimes you are only an observer, at other times you are involved intimately in other people's lives, but now as a mere recorder of events and personages, the shock of alienation arrived on me, yet deeper than that the ultimate intimacy of disparate lives.

Benny said that June's house was a well-seasoned, weathered cottage. His own deserted one had grown accustomed to rats; the dead people that had lived in the house, his parents, could often be heard arguing at night by passers-by. He only went up there by daylight to fodder the cattle. The hum of taped music drifted down from the hotel.

"They have everything at their fingertips above," he said pointing. "Take your money, boy, from whatever angle it's coming from."

He pulled out his pipe and knocked it off a stone. A cormorant flew by, its coarse black wings aflutter, beak like silver in the spring sun, that set now without the lake catching its reflection. For it was far west of the pines. Some people neglect their experiences by holding them at arm's length, at verbal distance. Not so Benny, his generosity of spirit was personal, abrupt. Behind us, June's three kids were playing, only one of whom I think resembled him. They were all beautifully turned out, like out of a bandbox, not a hair out of place. The eldest had straight black hair, gypsy-like, and seemed to reflect humorously on things. The youngest had fair curly locks, talked of TV programmes, wide astonished eyes, blue. The four-year-old had undistinguished auburn hair, colourless skin. She stood between us, intent upon the fishing and saying and interrupting all the beautiful encouraging things for life that a child can tell or repel.

The waves were heavy and cold as rock. Feeling was dispersed by the heart, intestines and lungs. Like embryos, sluggishly, drops of water broke away from under the ice and flowed, ice-covered. He, Benny, didn't turn round to look at the cars as I did. He gossiped away, cruel, erratic, interested in the beyond. As if he knew the laundered space of each guilty psyche, and how each family renews itself for the future. For though, over the past few months, myself and Benny may have dispensed with familiarity, except for the cheerful courtesies, all's well. For you see they had his house scourged for years, those amiable frightened men, but now seemingly all's settled. June has given him joy and sustenance, and she maintains an aura of doubtful reserve, and I don't see her any more.

The Island and the Calves

EASTER WEEK dragged on in the distant crowded church.

By the houses, too, the spiritual world was ecstatic and sensual. Jim felt he might lose control of each and every moment, deep bass music, The Seven Last Words of Jesus Christ on the Cross by Haydn, till ultimate flight and optimism. He had begun to name with awe each part of the outside world, gaining equilibrium. The early turbulence of wind and rain had deepened the reflections in the now calm lake, a sensual pike rose momentarily across the surface, spills appeared under the drying trees in the water. As if small fry were rising. The country Sussex house was packed with prams and children, wet dolls sat out under the birches, cows nudged at their fodder and drifted down to the unblossomed rhododendrons.

In the deep pool of water, the edges of the purple pines sharpened towards sunset.

Winds channelled through the woods with a low hum. The things that my soul refuses to touch are as my sorrowful meat, was Edward's cry. Down by the lake's edge Jim and Edward were walking. Edward was dressed like a Jew, woollen hat, scapular like a lanceolate that pierced his breast, and eyes so light a blue that the pupil might slip away, melt. And then the brooding irony of devotion. In him the body and soul were one. The actor's idea of the stage and its dimensions were present in his judgement of things. He had just arrived from Gloucester, thence from a further coastline where he and some friends had celebrated the real mass on a deserted beach. The priest was a social worker, the altar girls had tended to him, they craved poverty and the expression of their bodies, how you might never trust a crucifix, the Temple and the Holy Ghost were different but not too different, and Edward's speech concerned otherness and celebration.

They walked on Jim's land.

The figure of the young priest, as a ghost of modernity, walked between them.

16

By the flush of leaves and waves coming together, apart on the shore.

It would be unfair to show how much they loved each other, that would be to invade them; let their occupations this day speak for them.

Besides the odd human detail. They have, for old time's sake, erected an aerial off a high tree to pick up the Mass in Irish from Radio Eirinn, to allow the chants from Jim's home country to permeate the house. A minute's silence here is worth hours somewhere else in a year's time. The preciousness of this turbulence that is not fleeting. Not magic, but possession of something between the rhododendrons and the birch. Young willows flock in the hedges, the catkins have sprung furry with yellow combs. Edward will not listen or look at the trees or the water, all these images, the geranium and the lily have gone within, he has an ambiguous response to man's delight in nature, yet his ecstasy is not shortlived.

Jim burns with the necessity to get things done, a busy self, he perches on the shoulder of his friend looking at the competing world.

The house and the kitchen were wrecked by the chaotic night before, the children stepped over and added to the debris, babies crawled into cupboards, and a neighbour's child was studying the contents of a cardboard waste box. A young girl sat outside eating sand. Beside her, a crisp bag filled to bursting with primroses, thorns, pissmires. So, after their silent walk, the men set to work. That is, Jim washed and scrubbed the kitchen down while Edward talked with hardly credible gestures, or hardly heard what his friend answered, such was his zealous discovery of spiritual energy. He swaggered between the windows and the trees with chopped timber for a fire that was not burning. Popped large lumps of apple tart into his mouth. The radio was switched off during the priest's passionate ritual for the burial of Christ. The timorous martyrdom that crackled through space. In the silence came the sound of oars beating off a boat across the waters. A hare with long girl's thighs and legs stopped short of Jim in the garden.

He appraised the tension trembling in the hare's back, the jump withheld in the sockets of its knees; Jim had interrupted a joyous fling around the wild apple trees.

They looked at each and sauntered off to their various retreats.

Margaret was upstairs sleeping, tired from going to and fro in the world, and from walking up and down in it.

Last night she had screamed, Pain is practical, it's not something you go on and on with. For the men put no trust in their intelligence, expecting only to create well.

Now, today, she had been regretful, knowing how easy it is to inflict the truth on others without considering its possible repercussions on oneself. She listened to the two men downstairs, doubted her heroic capabilities, leaves sparkled on the walls around her. Haydn's music burst through into the final celebration. She was glad that the children had not surrendered to their conciliatory fathers, that she could read on without interruption.

Each morsel of food made her grow lightheaded. Her hair drifted across the pillow, her skin dried.

"Under the boardwalk, down by the sea," Edward was singing in a mock-Oxford accent for the barely interested children.

Now darkness. The much blessed body had been buried under the monolith of ritual, and so Edward brings his Bible in from the car. The coot and the sky-goat blow their horns over the purple lake. Closing the door, the inmates of the house, the trapped butterfly and the sleeping robin under the rafters, all heard the sudden mad screech of the geese rising with a chorus of screams, the lake suddenly fell sideways as they flew off. Emigration had begun. Edward read from the Old Testament, from Job and then from the Song of Songs, from the Natural Law in the Spiritual World, the everlasting kissing and fondling, how sweet the hoofs of the doe. While Jim imagined a priest in sleeveless leather donkey-jacket mounting the marble steps, where biblical vegetation was trapped, charcoal dirt on his arms, and then erratic improvisations in the organ loft.

The Song of Songs was Edward's place in time.

For him there was no need of externalizing the presence of God.

That was Edward's totality.

Yet, there remained the music of the ballet, unprecedented for Jim, and without such dancers, the song of the heart. He had followed the movements of the calves for no special reason, other than after wet nights when the wind ranged heavily, he would find them in different places under the hedges. Their farmer provided fodder for their travels. From the general sheet of cold he surmised that the wind one day came from the east. It drove manfully against the wall of the house, repeated itself in dreams, was present in water and in the ruddy veins of the child.

The calves were tucked in against the further ditch of the field. So that, too, was east for them, the nebula. Towards the stones of the Dogs mountains, under the plural form of myths, they had found refuge. During the night and the following day, rain fell harshly and at noon the wind softened, warmth resurrected, and he surmised from the south the wind came, it softened the eyes, the hair of Margaret, cooled the bushes. . . . The calves were now under the ash-and-willow hedge to the left of the unattended Holly Well; hiding from the warm bucketing wind, chopping, straying, pondering, the flaming calf in the lead, all the rest mottled black and white.

Always, one stood while the others rested their chilled hoofs, stared unblinkingly at all who passed.

Now Jim knew the four points of the compass from the wind and the calves, the corners of that elementary field he extended onto the lake to find direction from there. For then there were no books in the house, no radio to guide him. And what was permanent, what stood still, would always point in a different direction to the man or the bird always moving, recognizing and turning, lifted on a current of air. He moved the field mentally out onto the water, between those lines of white surf, sallied forth with those early calves onto the rushing waves from north, south, east and west.

And even though this was an emotional, fundamental fashion of discovery, yet when the wind died down (no west wind ever blew) and passion departed, when passion departed and reason returned to the branches of a tree separating the heavens and the earth, when he stood bewildered by the strange simplicity of the sorrowful day that follows the joyous day, when man's heart might take that agile journey towards always discovering anew, still the points of that compass held firm.

The edges ran sharply out onto the murky headlands, over beautiful, distressed places, tapered off on mountain peaks and toppled palings on hawk and pine heads, beyond what he could not get to the other side of, remaining here, always imagining.

Now for Edward, he places the field on this island, though in a further lake. It took this sunshine, calm waters and relentless perception. He boated out to the island, drew a map of it, the monastery walls, the nest of the heron was east, when his plan was finally completed. In a line east from the house on this particular day you had the red calf, the birch, the aerial, the hawk, the heron. Fossils he collected for charms, as in older times; the knowledge of structure went undisturbed. The purple of the waves stained their arms. History became the studying of disappearing softness, for hardness always remained, the most accessible material of man.

Here on the island he experienced the distance between the island and the field, the pleasure of nesting in the warmest part, like the calves. Where all the brilliant stones have been sketched upon by the bones of fish, shells of molluscs, cups of coral, the brains of kings and labourers. This island, morning receiver of gifts, plants and water, up where dawn's light had slipped from its chilled moorings and drifts among the tall heads of the spruces, where the herons are babbing, and where the deer once slept with its nose on its tail, closer to the Word, and no closer for all that energy spent.

The children screamed to be allowed on board, maddened by Jim oaring so constantly, seeking relief between home and the island, his pockets weighed down by stones, his hearing half-gone from the warfare of startled birds.

His house that day took on more and more the appearance of an abandoned novel, the children and he and Margaret could no longer sustain any kind of order. For at last he had authenticated the outside world, and each part was now sustained by itself and no longer needed a deity or an interpreter for a tiring audience. Into this house, then, as Margaret came down the stairs for a light supper, and the geese beat their way off in the appointed direction, Edward trustingly brought his Bible, sought solace, and then, un-prompted and sonorously, began his reading of the Song of Songs.

20

The Curse

THE CANAL comes from where I live, fast as horses, taking along the twisted leaves from the strange plants in the tropical garden that settled there after the last war. She goes under the church and takes the spire along a quarter of a mile. Next, is crushed by the walls of the mill that go up a hundred feet, so that she is brick-coloured and hampered by false rapids. The rats slide down the wheel and sometimes the army boys in their stiff boots pick them off with pellet guns.

Keenan's is on the bridge above.

And here we are like tadpoles in the water, but hardy and fine.

We are proud of the shape of ourselves, especially when one of us swims quick below in the shadow of the mill, darting through the other's legs like the perch that come up the canal in quiet schools, catapulting from deep hole to deep hole, weaving without moving.

But we keep to the shallow pool, where we can climb up onto the mossy wet walls and dangle our legs like white roots in the water.

The sun moves past like a big yellow cork, bobbing above and brightening the green beds. Each side of her is stiff and cold. The two boys go under to collect things, and stay down there bubbling away, to look up, as they beat backward with their soles at the flowing sky, as if the world had never happened. And when the girls arrive at three we will all drift under water, holding our breath, in a circle that drifts and shifts, till we surface with aching lungs, shooting up like people on springs.

Nobody comes here but ourselves.

Then suddenly, we are sitting on the wall, the new Triumph Herald, the first in the district that we have studied above in Kildare town, comes over the bridge, turns with a scream of wheels and crawls down the open path with its engine off. It is being steered by Pat Wheelan, a big likeable gauger, who comes from the Ring, same as my father. He is general dog's body for Ted

Webster-Smith, the horse-racing man who sits, wrapped in his tweeds in the passenger seat, smoking with the confidence of a man of the world.

They are just in off the Curragh.

Webster-Smith is the son of General Tom, who was buried along with his famous stallion, Tain Rue, but Ted only goes through the rudiments of horse-training. They sit in the car, with its flashing fins and wings, a moment talking, they look over at us, and we watch the two men wondering.

Next, they get out and we can hear them laughing behind the car, urging each other on. With Ted in bright togs and Whelan in his big drawers, they start running down to the canal.

Pat Whelan's belly bounces. "Is she warm?" he shouts over. We nod. The two men are so white that none of us wants to look at them. It seems that this is the first time they have ever had their clothes off, that their paunches have seen the light of day. Both have whiskey-red faces. They have no muscles. "How are you chaps?" Webster-Smith calls across, nearly as if he knew he was invading our territory. Then, at a signal, Webster-Smith leaps off the pavement stones into the canal at the deep part, and Pat Whelan, blessing himself, jumps in at the shallows.

They both hit the water like baby elephants, with great splashes and roars. The water level rises.

Pat Whelan gets out to jump in again.

He doesn't seem to mind that his drawers have fallen a little, so that his hairy arse is showing and when he turns around we can see his mickey, all shrivelled up with the water, like something made out of putty and not finished.

But undaunted, he hauls up his drawers and leaps in again with a painful belly flop.

Webster-Smith comes up on his back, spouting from the mouth and beating each side of him with his arms. He comes to his feet. "Not bad for an old fellow? Can you do that?" he calls across. We shake our heads. He repeats the performance, swallowing more water than he ought to, and when he again comes to his feet, we can see that his pot belly and thin chest are lined with red weals. He winks at us in a boyish fashion and goes under holding his nose, and next we can see Pat Whelan struggling where Webster-Smith

22

has got a hold of him. The two men fight and cheer and pull at each other, all as show for us, till they fall and go under. Next, Webster-Smith appears up-stream with Pat Whelan's drawers held aloft in his hand.

Then, poor Pat surfaces, blinded for air and spluttering, just as the girls come down the path, running with their towels. They want to know how long those big idiots are going to be here. We shrug. All Pat can do is squat in the water. Webster-Smith hauls himself out, goes to the car, "It's all yours, ladies," he says, passing, and begins drying his legs and shoulders with a towel big as a bedspread. His shoulders are thin and bent forward. He is laughing all the time at poor Pat who everybody knows is always trying to put on airs. And though it's true that Webster-Smith, despite his fortune, has never kept a decent horse, and because it's also true that my family tell me I will never grow a screed taller than I am, I turn to the boys and say, "Watch this," get up and cross to the car, which I admire as much as I can, running my finger over the wings, the bonnet, then, now. . . .

"Would you have a job out at the stables?" I ask.

"Are you like the rest," he says, "mad to be a jockey?"

"Yes, Mr Webster-Smith."

"And have you ever been up on a horse?" he asks.

He slops after-shave onto his chin and under his arms.

"Many times," I says.

Back behind us Whelan is growing hysterical as the girls approach the water.

"I'll give you a job," he decides, "if you'll do something for me."

"What's that?" I ask.

The girls skim the water like swallows.

"OK, Patrick," Webster-Smith shouts down, "I'm coming," and he saunters over and puts Whelan through further anguish by leaving his drawers on the bank out of reach, till the poor gauger, flushed and bad-tempered and naked as the day God made him, flounders up onto the shore and pulls on his wet drawers looking around to see if anyone would spite him. But the girls all look away and slip down-stream through the now quiet canal. Webster-Smith gives me two shillings, and with the extent of his laughing coughs up mucus against the back wheel of the car.

"Clear off," Whelan shouts at me, "and don't be annoying Mr Webster-Smith."

"I'm working for Mr Webster-Smith now," I says.

The two men look at each other a moment, then puzzled by the state of affairs Whelan goes behind the car to put on his clothes. Ted pulls a comb through his hair, looks into the rear-view mirror and makes a parting sharp as a knife-edge. He draws on his brown leather boots. "Right," he says, "give me a mo till I work something out."

I go down and pick up my clothes and the crowd follow and gather around, looking from the pair above to me and back again. "Where are you going?" Sally asks, looking over my shoulder. "I haven't a clue," I says, "but the next time you see me it'll be on the back of Sir Ivor booting for home." "Aye, aye, aye," the lads say, shifting uneasily in their loose togs. "Wait and see," I says. The boys beat the moss off their purple knees and elbows, trying to come to grips with my self-importance. "Well," says Sally, "wherever you are going, Mr Knowall, you had better be around for me at nine." "We'll see," I says.

The two men are waiting for me in the car.

I climb over into the back of the Triumph which is known to every pub in the district but still important for all that. The seat is filled with crops and other riding gear, and so big it is impossible to sit still, as we swing up and around the bridge, the radio, like a miracle, bursting forth with the turn of the ignition, and I know I am in a different world when so much can happen at the same moment in time. I put my hands each side of me for balance, except for one last wave at the gang below, still looking after us.

Pat Whelan tries to pretend to know everything by telling Webster-Smith of my name and age and background, and the fact that my father knows more about gardening than he does about horses. But Webster-Smith takes no interest.

We stop outside the Grenville Arms Hotel.

"Now, Charlie," he says to me, flicking back the wet hair out of his eyes, "go in those glass doors, through to the lounge, and past that into the residents' lounge. Get your bearings. You'll see a bloody little bitch behind the bar called Molly Burns, who keeps the travellers in drink till the small hours, but insults us locals. Do you know her?"

"I see her about town," I says.

"That's the one," confirms Whelan.

"Well, she has insulted me and my friend here," continues Webster-Smith, "and I want you to go up to her and say, 'You rotting cunting bitch', then clear off out of there." He studies me. "Have you got that?"

"Yes," says I, "and when do I get to ride the ponies?"

"We'll see," he says, "how you get on with this job first."

Webster-Smith gets out and tips his seat forward.

The minute I'm out of the car they accelerate across the road, turn and speed to Murphy's bar. I go up the steps cautiously, knowing their eyes are on me, and on in through the glass swing doors. Another world where I must pretend to be about some business. Along the soft carpet, feeling my wet feet slip along in my sandals. I step, remembering I have left my towel in the Triumph. On again. The knob of the door into the lounge turns around and around in my hand but won't open, till I have the common sense to push it on in. The Dean from the Deanery is sitting right inside taking his afternoon coffee with one of his aged parishioners. His strange eyes seem to bore into mine. "I'm looking for my father," I blurt out. He loses interest in me, and shakes his head sadly toward the lady. I am swallowed up by the airless music and the dim lighting, till I see a small corridor leading on into a further, smaller lounge in which there is no one. The place smells. Empty bottles and stained glasses on all the tables. I peer under the drop-leaf of the counter and see Molly Burns on her hands and knees, pushing a scrubbing brush over and back across the raw boards. I bend and stand behind her a few seconds, trying to get wind for the rhyme that is going over and over in my mind, thinking to myself, my chance has come. She seems to feel my presence behind her, and tugging at the mat under her knees, she comes off her haunches and turns, so that her glasses loosen. "You rottin' cuntin' bitch," I whisper and run without looking behind me. "Come back," I hear her shout. "What did you say?" And I flee past the pictures of famous horses, past the Dean, through the glass doors and out onto the street, over the road, till, breathless, I pin myself against Murphy's wall.

The men step down from the bench in the snug where they have been watching.

"You did what I asked?" asks Webster-Smith, steering me into the open bar.

"I did," I says.

Pat Whelan laughs and laughs till the tears run down his cheeks.

"And what," asks Webster-Smith, "did the dear lady say to that?"

"Nothing."

"Well, you are a good chap, Charlie."

"And when do I get to ride the horses?"

"We'll have to see," he says.

I stand there waiting while the joke is passed down the bar to the local gamblers who are listening to the radio. They laugh, as is expected of them, and shuffle their feet, and look bemused as Whelan slops his drink and repeats over and over what I told Molly Burns, "You dirty rottin' cunt," he says, "that will put manners on her, by Christ." I wait.

I can taste there in the air the sweet smell of weakness and failure. "Can I come out tomorrow?" I ask Webster-Smith. "No, not tomorrow," he says, looking ahead of him. "Thursday?" I ask. "No, not Thursday either," he answers, half to himself, but without impatience or embarrassment. "Don't be annoying Mr Webster-Smith," says Pat Whelan in a sharp whisper so that the others, in their long gaberdines, cannot hear.

The locals are going back to the racing pages, over the runners and riders where my name should one day be, and sometimes they call on Webster-Smith for his opinion, but only out of courtesy, then they disagree among each other all over again, as if driven into exaggeration by their inferiority.

I go as far as the door, thinking maybe Webster-Smith will take pity on me if I stand there long enough.

But purified by their sobering jump in the canal the pair go on drinking as if they didn't notice me.

At last, I turn one foot into the hall, open the outside door, and shout backward to all there, "You dirty fat English gets," and clear off up the street diagonally, thinking, if it comes to it, I can run forever. I hide in Farley's bakery and see Whelan appear. He

26

makes no attempt to follow me, but takes a stroll up and down outside the pub with a troubled look on his face, as if the life he has been leading has whittled away all his energy. Then he goes back in again. Minutes later the two men emerge, wait for Dunne's haulage to pass, then cross the street to the hotel to see the effects of my curse.

The Dean walks out, parts with his parishioner and salutes Webster-Smith, who speaks down to the little man for a few moments. The Dean takes stock of the evening sky, then turns toward St Brigid's. On his way he buys a half-pound of mushrooms, going up on his toes to check the scales. I decide that there is no use crying over the number of doors closed to me in that town from then on, so I accompany him, pretending, for today at least, to be other than I am, and much more besides, while he, thinking he knows me, talks of superior breeds in the sprinting world.

Blake's Column

I

A Tin of Sardines

Mr Humphries's Selected Essays, *which will certainly recommend him on Judgment Day to the Creator, may not succeed so well in our more petty habitation. I think he has settled for the well-turned phrase, rather than exert the imagination, so that what once ran cleanly through the ocean has been parboiled, salted, oiled and tinned, still it bears a very fine Christian label.*

We have need of such lies to sustain us through our drab inferiority. . . .

. . . Coming from Granard, loaves in a parcel, Ben hanging from the rafter, How do you know what you are coming home to or from, we are broken and have no words for this. This is forever. *An sios suas.* The greatest gift I have is the gift of forgetfulness, she whispers, On from Granard by train is best, he explains, for here, because the damn bus may never arrive. . . .

Mr Blake got up from his small table. It was seven in the morning and he was again caught between different destinies. Cattle were straddling the ditch in an attempt to find shelter from the sleet. Hills went off into the mist, and when they saw him, the young calves came up the frozen garden and licked the window panes, snorting at him inside.

When he bent forward they reared back in fear. He should not have moved like that, so quickly.

How suddenly all these beings had thrust themselves into his consciousness and as suddenly withdrawn, because, maybe, of his lack of sympathy. What might stay in opposition and never find a home. *Weaxan*/grow. Mr Blake stood a long time there looking out, his two hands stuck in his jacket pockets, finishing with a flourish what he had not yet begun.

II

The bicycle shop was a vast open space with forms and benches and a drip from the roof that ran down the oily bricks.

On the bench under the old leaded windows, Mr Blake, the well-known columnist, fell into a fit of coughing.

This ended a long and joyous reverie considering the faults of a certain play of his and questioning the reasons why people had praised it when it first appeared, 14 August 1972. Like all others of his creed he was superficially hardened toward unhelpful criticism, but especially anxious over praise which he had not earned. The bicycle-man came over to see was he OK, but backed away from the combination of Vic and garlic.

The bout of coughing sent jarred images of Mr Blake's contemporaries before his eyes, and for a moment he was defenceless. . . .

"I'm all right," he sniffed, "a certain cunt of an actor just went the wrong way."

"That so," said the bicycle-man, returning to the *Evening Herald*.

If he was to persist with this line of questioning, Mr Blake's wits told him, he might render himself insane. Worse still, he hated the language in which this barrage of guilt presented itself. I must get out of this, he thought, this internal humiliation —

"Goodnight, Henry."

"Goodnight."

He wiped his eyes and mouth and wheeled his bike up the village, loath to go home. But fortunately he spied two cars of well-known solicitors parked by the village pub. He entered unobtrusively and ordered an orange. The three men were sitting among the peasant furniture, well inebriated, and dressed to the nines. He saluted them, but beyond the usual formalities, he could tell they did not want his company. He persisted. "Slumming?" he asked. Two of the men smiled, the other continued talking, except for the odd backward look of the eye. "Look," said the talker, Jack Small, turning on a further interruption, "We are having a private conversation, all right?" Mr Blake knew domestic trouble when he saw it, so he plucked the folds of his trousers into his socks, rode home the country road, lungs and heart free from alcohol and cigarettes, and in compliance with the dictates of his column (you might say, he thought) began that night a series of features on certain figures in the trade union world, beginning with *real* notes collected on the factory floor, then to the *unreal*, speeches from the politicians and the like, on to the *ambivalent*, meaning the employers, and finally, the *fatalists*, the union leaders.

He tried to cease from interpretation when he wrote, seeking as far as he could to create, but for the moment creation had become abuse against those he considered self-seeking, including trade-union officials, junior and senior, who over the years had given him important information. And knowing, as he wrote these rebukes to people who had trusted him, that he was cutting all ties with security, Mr Blake assured himself, Yes, sir, this is only the beginning, for even if he were left with only gossip to glean from, then he could move toward an ever more formidable betrayal.

III

Chapter 15

The fields were sodden with melting snow and the gutters full. All morning there was the unceasing slap of water on the streets of the town. He walked through the brilliant morning carrying a sack on his back. In it was the body of his child. He thought this was the case, to let him grow cold on his back. His father-in-law watched him through a slit in the curtain pass by.

A great deal of the tension had died in him and now he could feel every cold inch of his body. Some knew of his recent distress and others didn't, but only towards evening did someone say, "Ah mister, mister, why don't you go back to the house?"

"I think I'll stay down a while longer," he said. "I'll not go up the hill yet."

How your face froze! How the lines gathered! A fight in Bridge Street. In summer, here, a thunderstorm. To start again at the morning, he walked in the road from the lakes, and did the usual things of the single walker. Xmas lights glittered in every window, unsafe lights in the early morning.

As he came in Farnham Road, soft pellets of rain sharpened his brow. The sack he covered with his coat and his face froze.

"You're out early," Mr Jenkins, the solicitor said. He was walking his Great Dane and was clothed in a heavy green Aran jumper and wellingtons.

"I was thinking just now of that dog," the man replied.

They walked together along the railway track, whistling to the dog and thinking their separate thoughts. In the town, bottles were sprayed across the streets from the night before. What he looked forward to was spontaneity, even for the carcass he carried on his back. The people had worn it thin, the spontaneous love.

"This morning," said Mr Jenkins and his fingers shaking, "this morning, rummaging around the old house among my mother's things, I opened a bag and found. . ."

Birds flitted about the old Abbey in which Owen Roe rested, his poisoned intestine blistering the coffin.

The moon was a disc slanted and thrown off into the distance.

Now, last night and the night before, what great things did I dream? Sharpest dream of all to see the child wounded in the neck by an arrow. His hands tugging at the arrow. And the man's wife saying, We will always be leaving by different doors and he answering, OK, that's OK, I wouldn't change it for the world. . . .

". . . and palms leaves if you don't mind."

The rain barrels were drumming throughout the town.

But to begin again at the morning when he had awoken as the waves beat a slow retreat from his door, she said, This lack of affection between us must cease, for we mean everything to each other since everything is so vague and unfamiliar. This absurd lack of affection. He lifted his son onto his back. He kicked back the wet grass across the fields. He strolled into town.

IV

Dublin

Dear John,

I feel that whatever your intentions, the form of muckraking you are now at in the dailies seems to be saying, Look! Look! How good I am! Soon no one will care what you have to say. I am terrified of meeting any of our old friends. You know I will always respect you and I do not mean to be cruel.

I expect you do at least eat well. Ben has grown big as a house and plays chess with his friends.

I think you began as a dreamer but developed other conceits. Why don't you begin again in strange surroundings. That place is no good for you.

With winter here, the dress trade has gone slack, but Mother is nothing but encouragement. Maybe you should return to the city, for we both know what isolation can inflict on a body. Wishing you well, oh yes, I was attacked and robbed of my handbag on the way home in Donnybrook, of all places, the other night. I am without the gold chain, as for the money it means nothing. The police were less efficient than the lads, one of whom said, It's all right Mrs, threw me against a signpost and whipped the bag. I was screaming and screaming, but no one came. But I am all right now.

Love Sheila.

PS   My drama teacher says I have the right voice for the wrong century. Yesterday I read "The Overcoat" by Gogol. I miss the country but Mother says we can't go down till summer. See you then.

Ben.

V

With Sheila's house coat around him, Mr Blake was full pelt at it with the bellows. Smoke poured through the kitchen. He cursed and swore. Then at last he did what he should have done in the first place, opened the flues and collected the soot. Steam poured from the wet ash, but the fire grew and smoke poured out the open door, over the frosty roofs of the dreary outhouses.

Then he returned to his writing.

Blake's Column

John Blake was a small, feverish man with red, seedy cheeks. Sheila and Ben had left him a year and a half ago. Because. Because. He now lived in the cottage alone, taking his morning walk at cock-crow, with the collar of his coat up to his ears and taking in all he heard. They had moved into the cottage three years ago after a lifetime in the city, but he had been born near here. At seven, years ago, spent six months on his back in the local sanatorium. Gone to school over the road. Next, the diocesan boarding school, and after that, two years in an insurance office where the underwriter in the motor section cut all his letters by half until he learned to convey only what was important.

By night he now ploughed into the private journal that took up his whole life. The journal had once been his master. Now that he was alone, it was his companion.

And through it he tried to fight off the mindlessness of fourteen years in a newspaper office.

The wind roared from the south-east.

He dropped his column off at a post office run by three orphaned daughters.

From Wednesday to Friday he stopped over in Dublin at an old associate's flat. The rest of the week he spent here, in The Valley, an old cottage rebuilt with broad-flanched chimneys, floors of patio slates cemented into stone, walls of rusty brickwork with hangings from Colombia, the windows austere and tight against the wind, but because some of the rooms were only half finished, he lived in the kitchen and slept bundled up in blue rugs in the child's room above, next to the immersion heater.

In summer, sweet pea climbed across the iron trellis of the porch. And come spring, the daffodils returned in tight clumps, then bunches of Herb Robert that remained till autumn.

Like all those who live in the country, but whose minds are elsewhere, he never exercised his intelligence among the country folk but adopted a distant role, accepting their folkish advices and repetitive narratives, but today of all days he stopped the Pools collector as they went up the lane together and said, "Take our Minister, for instance."

"Yes," said Brennan.

"Minister of the Environment, born in Corlurgan, yes?"

"True for you."

"This is what happened. He told me himself. As a whipper-snapper, himself and the boys knew old Ferguson, yes, who had no indoor toilet and each day slipped down to the ditch to shit into the drain. He had a reliable branch there he used to hang out of. Well, your Minister went down there, nicked the stick with his pen-knife. The boys hid and waited. Old Ferguson came and let his trousers down, swung out over his deposit and down he went. I ask you."

"Boys will be boys," answered Brennan.

"You're not concerned that this man is responsible for the welfare of the country?" asked Blake.

"Makes no difference."

So Blake was forced into further coloured reproofs that got nowhere. "I must be about my calls. Good day, John," said Brennan, who tipped off up a garden path, his briefcase hanging loosely from his left hand. "See you tomorrow," Blake shouted after him. Brennan put his thumb up without turning round.

VI

An Attack on Virginity

I have made my laborious way through Mr Arthur Beymont's book recently, a man who relishes the socialist cause with an innocence tantamount to virginity. It seems to me a lot of horse shit, or excuse me, apocryphal ravings, to believe that socialism has yet to come. It is already here, and we must get on with what we have. A writer like this could not sustain his confidence for the length of his breakfast, never mind a book, but our socialist press will continue to present us with feeble English thinkers, rather than pay a good translator to give us the masters.

The other books of the month bring no surprises, unless you think of living as a life sentence, which most of the Irish do. Mr Eugene Williams will go on and on about the bric-à-brac of childhood, not a day's sickness, inverting Gogol's style who knew a stranger when he saw one. And Mr Sampson, please do not think otherwise, you are a yes-man, no matter the number of negatives you employ. Brendan Little continues to whine with the authentic cries of a drowning cat, albeit it with more style. And Mr Butane, if you persist in telling us of your dear Aunt Helen from Sligo, I will personally take a pistol to the principality of Monaco and shoot you.

In the other fields, politics for instance, O'Neill has us back where we started, thinking Union with Britain is a superior breed of union than Union with Ireland, for a people who are wanted by neither, except by him and for his own reasons. As he deals with women in his private life, so he deals with politics, gets into bed with all of them to prove his devotion to his wife. And as for the editors of this paper, who think Union with the Republic is the be all and end all, it seems the twentieth century has passed them by. Because the Irish have no idealism, they chose Republicanism, yet this fight started out over work and wages, not nationhood. A life in Insurance terms is worth what? £40,000 (with inflation)? With these sums we could be laying the foundation stones of small factories. Each life has a monetary value, but not in Unionism, Protestant or Catholic, so, would the gentleman who pays me for my piece please refrain from his ecstatic mumblings (I hear talk of his inserting a photograph of himself alongside), so that the cartoonists might have peace of mind. I might add that I think I am suffering from a failure of nerve. But I intend to write more of that in the future.

VII

Mr Blake was out feeding the finches in the crackling snow and sunlight when Mrs Robinson from the cocktail circuit directed her car down the lane. This was indeed a surprise. Knowing his tantrums, she parked nose-up against the gate and let herself into the house. By the repeated acceleration when the car stopped he knew it was she trying to wrestle her way out of the car with the ignition still on.

He piled the fat with the crumbs, sucked his frozen fingers and looked through the window to see what she was at.

Mrs Robinson was peering at the page in his typewriter.

He scooted round to the front of the house, took two deep breaths, and leaped into the kitchen.

Mrs Robinson was sitting in his armchair by the range, the kettle in her hand.

"Ah, it's you," she said, smiling.

"It is me," he replied.

She put the kettle on the open range, patted her lap and drew out a cheap cigarette. "I have news for you," she continued. "You and I have guests this evening."

"At your place?" he asked.

"Nowhere else, to be sure," as always calling on the uncalled-for certitude. "You'll come?"

"I will, if I'm allowed to get a bit of work done around here."

"Of course, dear." She tapped her cigarette into one of the cooking rings. "And your wife?"

"Mrs Robinson," he said evenly.

"Yes, John."

"Why do you continually ask after my wife? My wife has left me."

"We live in hope, John."

She stayed a half-hour, enjoying the heat and casting aspersions on the filth around her by adding to it. He went about his business, trucking in with wood and turf, then aired his feet before the fire. My God, she thought. His toes looked like they had been soaped in mud, then crookedly bent forward as if they might crawl off in shame. This was a pleasure Blake enjoyed.

"I have brought you a present," said Mrs Robinson.

"Aha?"

She took out a muslin bag of curried seal meat, which the two of them tugged and chewed with their milkless tea. It was delicious. Not bad at all. Excellent. Then Blake unearthed a jar of mussels. Oh vinegar. It suffices. Through the window the calves, half-hidden by the fossilized prints of their tongues on the glass, looked in and wandered off uncertainly, this being the first day of snow they had seen. A chain-saw buzzed near by, leaving a gap in the sky and when the scream of the blade died, the bell of the saw continued on.

"Well then, can you. . . ?"

So, Mr Blake stepped over the snow and, watched by Mrs Robinson, he drove the car into his yard and turned it, so that it faced back up the lane. Pulling on her gloves, she drove in first over and out of sight, disappearing with a loud bark of her horn as she hit the main road. Tractors pulled into the ditches to let her by and her small Morris was followed by all the dogs of the townland.

VIII

Chapter 17

I break into a run after all the others. Though my soul won't catch them. Not during the long jealous hours of daylight or the short fretful minutes of the night. There is an enemy sleeping with me. Like me in every movement. But I brighten and rise to walk over the splink in the fog curled round the few hazy lights of the man Brennan who lives haphazardly on his own and makes fortunes for others that he might increase his own by a ha'pennyworth, and behind him another, and behind him another with his suffering sister, their lights all on in the early morning, the sister's brother crossing the one field they all share in the fog, caught between going and coming by the bare pattern at his feet, carrying timber and cardboard, stopping for the traffic of morning sounds, knocking on his neighbour's council door till he drops his head for the answer within, and out it comes, exaggerated by the early muffled light and the horn of the sun, "Yes, yes, just a minute, Henry," a chair disturbed and a cigarette dropped into the ashes of the holly and cherry trees, the two men finish the bottle of port and watch me swim past through the wet bushes toward your kitchen where none have yet been to bed, I'm relieved to see you, but then I know you are not up alone, "Here he is," he says, "It's in his cup," the fortuneteller tells the company gathered, "That fellow there, for him it's here at the bottom, he is cursed with the sickle and the sword, aye," James the fortuneteller, delighted with the extent of my innocence, laughs across my head, "He has many enemies, aye, and they are telling lies on him." Everywhere in the room and beyond is the sweet chorus of the partriarchal instruments. James steps toward the muddy, unimportant hay, like me in every movement. "Will I sleep with him sometime?" you ask, "Whenever you wish," I answer, and outside the three men and the single sister are crossing and recrossing their field, heating up their prefabricated tigins with debris

37

from the ditches, sallies and shavings, their voices warm as
thrushes' eggs, carrying bread and milk, light timber and
cardboard, reading out the Garda summons over the last jet of
gas and burdened with hunger that slights them, "Are you'se
off to school?" James the fortuneteller shouts from his perch
in the lofty barn after the dead postmistress's daughters as
they saunter into town. Then the sister comes to scold the men
and rifle their pockets for the evening meal.

IX

It was a bad day for Mr Blake. Nothing went right from the
beginning. The electric pump had frozen. He could no longer write
because nothing came and he stopped above in the child's small
bed, freezing and hungry. All his colossal arguments had deserted
him, and he longed to hear someone down in the yard.

In the afternoon he heard the cry of the beagles coming from the
direction of the lake. He ran down in his dressing-gown in time to
see the fox dart across his frozen garden, minutes later followed by
the dogs. The men came up, undid the two gates and streamed
through without a by-your-leave. From the other window he saw
the fox flying along the hill toward the village. Then, Mr Blake
dressed and, fighting a desire to hide above in the bed again, he ate
a breakfast of cold porridge and honey, heated up a pot of rainwater
over the gas and bathed his piles. He was squatting like that, over
the saucepan, in the centre of the kitchen floor when his brother-in-
law came to collect him. It was an embarrassing moment when he
saw the uncomprehending face at the window.

He let his brother-in-law in.

"No, not that," Mr Blake shook his head, "But I am afflicted by
haemorrhoids."

"Well," said James, his brother-in-law, "it was not a pretty
sight."

"Not mad yet."

"Catch you."

They walked up onto the road and waited for the taxi from
Smith's. While they waited his brother-in-law read his hand,
rubbing his thumb over and back across the wrinkled palm. But
before he could hear his fortune, Smith came over the brow in his

Datsun. They drove first to Percy's where John-Pat was collected, onto Bridie's for Hughy, then to PJ's who was waiting at the door, back up across the tortuous hills in the crowded car while Smith kept up a harangue against the cost of doctors and prescriptions. They pulled into a side road to avoid a funeral coming from the other direction. Then reaching the town they all went their various ways, to meet again by the monument at eleven, where Smith would fume and rage as the clock wound toward midnight, and the countrymen would not appear having found after-hours drinking in the lax hostelries of the area, and when they did come, piled high with parcels of bread and tea and butter, Smith would speak ne'er a word to anyone, but pull away from each dropping point with an angry acceleration, "And if you did not speak up," the brother-in-law had it, "he would fly past your fucking door." Then finally dropping off Blake, who was always last and soberer than the rest, Smith would whine, "Now, Boss, you see what I have to deal with, day in, day out," as he held each pound note up to the light. And arriving back after his day on the town, Blake would look over his journal and feel appalled, powerless to justify his existence, till he obliterated all his weaknesses and censured the living past.

X

I detect in myself someone who would own up to another's crime so my own might be considered and my fame increased accordingly. No hint of flesh or hair could persuade me that I existed at twenty, nor companion at forty give evidence of my worth. Nor could I defend myself from reality, when, as some part of me chooses to consider the exciting and deepening possibilities of my life ahead, there for one terrifying moment remains only my life before. And from these unwilled insights, emerges myself, unwilled, judged, unreasonable, and from this flow the lives of other people.

XI

The bus ride to Dublin was a cold, cheerless affair. He changed at the outskirts to a 54. The familiar city instilled a certain hopefulness, that was always followed by sentimentality as the bus chose to pass the house where Sheila and Ben lived, out of their element, trying to deal with meaningless exchanges. He searched the street for a sign of any of his family. No one. The hedge newly shorn and the clay turned up and dug for spring. A green bag of Irish peat at the left side of the door unopened. A Chinese lantern hanging over the pale blinds of the living-room. The bus got by the road-works and wheeled on into the midday traffic and Mr Blake looked ahead, oblivious to the "request" programme pounding through the radio speakers, but listened, instead, for the bus operator's gargled voice interrupting the station with organizational trivia, like a voice at sea keeping contact with lost souls, and he was glad when their driver was called on to answer and give his position, twice, because of bad reception. And he was delighted, too, to find that his stern brogues and heavy coat were of more durable quality than those worn by his superiors at the newspaper office. The editor appeared at his desk, complete with crumbs on his lips from an overwrought lunch. Mr Blake argued the toss with him, and leaving, tried as best he could to avoid the new journalistic successes, female and male, who sat perched by their typewriters, sounding like daft parrots, as they whittled away at their self-infatuation, till they too might end up like him, rearranging the editor's words in his ears. . . . "The best thing for you, John, might be to open a small business," he smiles, "a restaurant."

"Aye," answers Blake, knowing his place.

"There is money in it," he continues, "mark my words. Then you can poison them all at will." He throws back the sheets. "I can't use these."

Blake puts them back in his briefcase.

"Don't take it personal."

"My cheque?"

"At the desk as usual."

To the library. But Blake could not settle there for long. He phoned Sheila, but received no reply, then got through to Freeman who told him that his bed was there as usual. He bought his herbs and spices, his dried fruit and wholemeal. Fled from corner to corner in the rain and met Freeman at last, just when his patience could no longer sustain him across known thoroughfares, pretending to a course of action, he adrift from his moorings, at the corner of Eccles Street. There was much to talk about. Freeman had no illusions and was of happy, warped nature.

"You've set the cat among the pigeons, Johnny, my boy," he said, "but it's only literary stuff. You don't fool me."

"I didn't think for a moment that I would."

"Are you still off dainties and on a herring?"

"I'll manage a pint."

Again he phoned Sheila, and when she replied, he had nothing to say for himself except to ask after Ben, who came on and described with accurate and bloody details a fall from a tree. She, too, offered him a room, and his sleep that night centred around a review he had written earlier in the week of a book of essays by Humphries, an egotistical man, who had befriended him in earlier days. His review, he hoped, had been noncommittal. Those who did not want to hurt the writer in question had returned the review. But now, in his dream, he saw that the writer was dead, laid out in his tweeds, his red hair bleached by the light, his thin feminine hands each side of him, dark eyes looking around, a hint of alcohol on his lower lip. His left eyelash stirred like a bird, balancing. Humphries was dead but kept looking around. Mr Blake, much younger here than his years, took him by the hand and led the distressed writer a few turns round the room. Humphries moaned and moaned.

He jumped at sudden noises, was obviously distressed and clearly dead.

Mr Blake awoke in the dead room, a pale blue light was flickering on Ben's woollen scarf that hung over the single item of furniture, a King Edward chair.

He woke full of love to find that Sheila and Ben were sleeping in the room just across from him. He was filled with excitement and longing that after a while passed. He thought of himself and Humphries, and of his many friends who were like that, feeling they were leading a dead man around the room, a turn or two, before he would lie down and die. Of them all he loved this writer best. He got up and dressed himself, turned up the collar of his coat and made for the bus without disturbing any in the house, because he should not have come there in the first place. The calves, he told himself would have broken through into his garden. Blake made many excuses to himself. He and two others were the solitary passengers, and on his way home he bewailed writers undone by fawners, who in their need sought religious or spiritual advantage, ravaging the emotions of their families, rather than deal with what their uncomplicated senses told them.

He prayed that he would not in time give in to extreme disorders, that the task he had set himself might prove fruitful.

In such hope Mr Blake spent his days.

The Girl in the Muslin Dress

MOODY ALEX, was singing "Under Milk Wood" to an old Welsh air she had learned from her grandfather.

Aimless lighting hung unhealthily from the glazed street corners, signs swung a little, the wind was strong enough. And I felt more tired now than ever before and could have sworn the rain, as it hopped off the bonnets of the cars, was speaking of something that happened in October. And then the alleys, crowding with the ghosts of gossiping women, talked of the secret life in England and lifted their skirts for all the world to see till, tiring of the orchestra, I pulled the hood of my duffle coat down tight, shutting out all the insistent voices, muffling the sounds of my steps.

Alex, walking way out in front with her sharp, strained assault, disappeared.

In panic, I lengthened my stride to a near run till I had her in sight again. You could hear the rumble of late and early trains thundering across the tops of the houses and my shoes were letting in both back and front, not at all the ding-dong business walking is for other fortunate gentlemen of the metropolis. Only for a certain softness of the head I might have discarded the shoes and gone barefoot, paddling along on my misshapen feet to Victoria and Pimlico, even further. But some loyal, affected passion deterred me from abandoning them in a strange parish. Standing in a doorway to light a cigarette, my life a matter of distances and disguises, I felt the racking, nimble drug suddenly move in the blood.

Around us the city was coming up for air.

Whole streets moved into focus, filled with washed-out colours and, looking up, I childishly felt the helter-skelter of the rain on my face and saw the dark clouds separate slowly under the coarse morning light. Above the shops, the skyscrapers, with certain hazy lights left on overnight, shoulder to shoulder stepped it down the sky. And I was badly thinking of lying in the thousand strange beds of Alex, old English lavender, hyacinths before rain, till in the

43

moonless night exhaustion and relief might finally coax both of us away, worlds apart.

Up ahead from me she stopped and disappeared into the doorway of a chemist's shop. I approached her expectantly but always looking hard ahead as if I hadn't seen this change in strategy. She had sat down against the door and was flicking the wet hair out of her eyes. I came and stopped and looked at her a while and went in and sat down beside her. "I know it's coming," she said.

It was a whole little world in that doorway. Her body was cold and wet, even the wind could not smuggle some colour into her bloodless cheeks. "I was beginning to lose you back there," I whispered. "It goes on and on," she said and we gave way our tempers for that kind salvation, touched hands a bit while the rain beat down on those blue-grey tiles just short of our outstretched feet.

A draught blew straight out from under the door and we had to shift tiredly about trying to avoid it but found our places, hunched up together, eventually.

Sleep, girl, sleep. I nursed Alex in my arms. It was coming up to six o'clock a church-bell said, repeating itself above the pious saplings and humid stones. She cursed under her breath. I don't know who, someone out there where dreaming happens, perhaps myself. The days pass.

"Look," said Alex. A timid-looking man in jamboree had come round the corner of the street opposite, carrying a large box against his chest which he set down against the closed gates of an underground station. This intoning man, dressed out in a squat yellow cape with a beret pulled down over his ears, disappeared round the corner and returned a long time later with another large box and a smaller one. Music could be heard like a serinette for the lifeless city and everywhere the rain was falling flat out from a great height down the grey sky, thousands of well-wishers, till they sputtered out on the broad swerve of the roadway. The reverent shook the bitter rain from his head and set the two large boxes together in a daft fashion, shoving the smaller one underneath. From inside his dripping coat he took a sheet of polythene which he quickly folded over the lids to protect them against the rain. He seemed satisfied enough and secured the ends of the polythene with some stones which he always carried for that purpose. Then he gathered himself up against the jagged gateway, shoved his hands deep into his pockets and, grimacing a bit, peered up and down the street, kicking back with his left foot.

He hummed a number of ancient concert-hall tunes. Meanwhile a dapper black man went by on a bicycle, wearing an Indian hat and a white coat down past his ankles. He was swerving from side to side and laughing ridiculously to himself in a plaintive, nearly familiar, manner. Like the ribald winos under a tree in summer. The man at the station shook his head sadly and turned and rattled the gates, taking a dekko this way and that down the length of the deserted station. Once, he seemed to make his mind up about something and went over and urinated in a corner, shaking his leg afterwards like a spare limb. A blue van came quickly down the street, throwing up arcs of rain-water on each side like the swish of the Spanish dancer's dress. It parked outside the station for some ten minutes, the engine running, the wipers working like mad and feet moved over and back below the level of the van. Then, by hap, a railwayman, dressed in peaked cap and stiff dark mackintosh drawn to the chin, smoked carefully over the puddles and joined the others out of sight.

When at last the van drew away after the democracies of the early morning, the boxes had been transformed by a multicoloured collection of newspapers and demotic magazines which the man viewed from all angles, the sky-washed polythene pulled across them, the brazen headlines sheltered in iron frames. The gates were open and voices echoed out from the windy station. The newspaper-man sat within on the smaller box, his legs crossed as he smoked, tapping out in mid-air a fair representation of a circle with his raised toe. Alex and I struggled up out of the doorway, hitching up our wet clothes and shivering, and then we crossed the road by the subway, the wind getting up so heavy down there that we held each other distastefully till we resurfaced a few feet from the newspaper-man, outside Hanger Lane.

"Christ, it's Sunday."

"I don't know, mate. I don't know why I'm here or what's coming over this country. The birds can explain. It used to be a picnic once upon a time but it's been downhill all the way since the war. Put them out of their misery, I say."

The pink night was dying out. Rendezvous would be made here later. We tiptoed past the ticket-collector's office. He was inside, engrossed in lighting up an evil-smelling oil fire with his back turned to wave the wand. In the slightly drunk office, a faded soap-calendar from 1939. Among the posters on the walls for sorrow, a distant picture of Alex would soon appear, an advertisement for a shorthand and typing firm in which she wears a wig after the operation when those intuitive lights dulled. Pass by. We made it down to the open-air platform unseen while up at the entrance the newspaper-man, after watching the manoeuvre, the mint from her dresses, gave us the thumbs-up sign long after we had gone from view. The two of us sat huddled up on a bench, the sky full of metal beams and wet glass where the riffraff, the sweet-papers and coupons ducked their heads and scattered, sailing right out of sight above the delving trees. When the first train came up the line for reveille and stopped like the end of the world, the pair of us collapsed into an empty, scrubbed apartment, drunk from tiredness, savouring the soft feel and warmth of the cushioned seats.

"I can feel it coming on," said Alex. "I'm afraid."

"I'll get you home," I said.

And Alex slept again though she might dart awake and look around as we hurtled to a stop in the various stations where Sally with the tortured legs and wearing the muslin dress had flown to work each morning in the kindly Indian engine-driver's cab, holding on for dear life in the musky, electric tunnels till that man had got switched to a different line.

It was a dull grey morning when we emerged in Pimlico. We passed the wrestling school and the creamy house of the mediums. And sometimes we could hear the parable of the Flying Oats blow up the gliding streets from the round world of the fly-overs, the pigeons picking themselves up with grave dignity from a roof of verdigris on a cinema. The streets themselves were empty and grey, all except for a few lone Queen hustlers who made their way giddily along the pavements, their make-up withered, ashen faced, looking round behind them now and then. "Penny for your thoughts," said these friends slipping by. And I did a nice 1920's shuffle with the aged boots in reply, a rendering the father had taught me on the kitchen floor. "My, my," they said, skipping away. Alex and I walking together now. We had begun talking in a slow, effortless manner, mixing up all kinds of words, faint-hearted, Alex's eyes so tired now, burned down to a hollow darkness.

She hesitated at the steps of a tall staid Victorian building. Come on. But she was watching slowly, moving back. The dull night-light had been left on and behind the wavering glass panels of the glass door it seemed that all the walls and, even further back, the domed ceiling, were covered with flowers. The cheerful, fragrant inside of a flower shop. We climbed the steps and looked in, glancing round with wonder. Hundreds of rich flowers, long green stalks going this way and that, a crevice of weeds, roses and tulips, strange wonders crowded the walls. And now they were murals which must have taken years upon years to paint. Jabbering excitedly, we suddenly backed away in fright as a huge round face appeared behind the glass, a Leviathan of a man looked out at us with curiosity, speaking away. He smiled with some kind of recognition, then these enormous hands turned the key in the lock, the door opened, the drug stalled.

"You like the painting?" he said in a choked, foreign accent, his hands demonstrating the ease of paint brushes.

"Yes. Yes."

He shook those paint-stained hands of his again and, touching Alex's hair with a finger, knocked away a bead of rain.

"Tsh. Tsh. Come from the rain."

We followed him in gratefully. The place smelled fresh and warm, it could have been a hospital yet there was no hint of the claustrophobic or disinfectant aura of those houses of rest from the streets. He took great satisfaction in pointing out all the flowers lying this way and that in the breeze, tucking a wing away here, a petal there. "Kan . . . Kan . . . Ka . . . Ka," he said with a hand describing his seaman's breast, swaying his arm like Queequeg poised to take the long fall with the harpoon. "I am Kanka." "What?" asked Alex fretfully, "what did you say?" "Name," he said with the same mattoid antics as before, "name is Kanka." "Oh," said Alex and we laughed and she understood this strange, radiant giant and her eyes lit up and she told him our names and he nodded his huge head firmly at each syllable and said both names with a gentle assurance, copying her Welsh pronunciation with an easy accuracy, his head cocked to one side as if he was listening to something far off.

Above our heads could be heard the children's voices and tiny feet padding over and back.

"The little one's awake. Come below. I have tea."

"Well, it's. . . ."

"Come."

Alex, fearing for her sanity, dug her nails into the back of my hand. Then she nodded.

We followed his great bulk down the herbal galaxy. He could scarcely fit between the bannister and the wall but hopped along nimbly enough, carrying his great weight with apparent ease. His child-cotton shirt round the armpits and down the small of his back was drenched with sweat and with his every movement, muscles turning to fat rippled the length of his body. On the ground floor, as we walked along a soft-coloured corridor, he stopped beside a plastic curtain hung from a short railing. "I show you what Kanka loves." He pulled back the curtain and there was a fresh, glowing shower-room, complete with drape-like towels, back-brushes and lilac soap. He sort of skipped into the shower and pivoting dextrously on his toes and heels, showed us how he scrubbed himself, giving off a pretence of girlish satisfaction at the feel of unseen water, his eyes shut, one little finger flicking imaginary soap out of his ear.

"Three, four times each night," he beamed, his breath tasting of pastilles.

He opened another door and we were met with a tremendous blast of heat and light, two immense oil-furnaces ran the length of the room. He opened one of the furnace-doors and gestured within to the frantic, sanguine balls of fire and he showed the thermometers and the brass fittings with an air of importance, brushing the pan-pipes with his sleeve to bring up a shine. "My work." He sat into an enormous, swaying armchair filled with all kinds of soft, colourful cushions and talked while he drank from mugs he had placed on fine-woven Turkish mats. From a slender box underneath the table where the empty, bleached bones of a fish lay, he extracted a large envelope from which he in turn extracted an old mnemonic poster with loving care, which he carefully spread across the table. He wiped down the upturned corners, turning his head sideways and, with his fingers, imitating the falling of tears. On the poster was a picture of furnace-man Kanka, dressed in a loin-cloth with four leopard-skinned ladies on his shoulders in the shape of a pyramid.

A nurse led in a pale-faced, smiling child in pyjamas, who sat up on his knee.

"Since the war, yes, I spent thirty-one years here with the children, night after night. England has been kind to me. Before, I travel the world with the circus."

"Look," said Kanka secretively to the child and drew up his sleeve and flexed his muscle, a small foreign Christ in an oleograph behind his head, the bend of his arm a small bed for the child who nipped him on the stomach. Kanka closed his eyes, talking, turning in the flap of the canvas tent, the mad ponies from Ankara steaming after the run, the heavy lion-smell from the cages, the women who drank with him swinging out of danger, the Moroccan dwarf who sat on his knee like this tousled child and smoked kif, puffing away like a steamer, talking of Mecknes and Fes and the cooling sherbet and a thousand others, nearly out of reach of his placid mind.

"The war, you see. Every night I am warm and wash." He shook his hand behind his back, imitating the action of the brush in the shower and. . . .

"You must go now," he said, bitterly. "It's like lies, lies, lies."

Alex nervously jumped to her feet.

He and the child, aloft on his shoulder, left us to the back door where we climbed clumsily among the cold church-goers.

Leaving the lightsome hospital behind, Alex put her head on my shoulder and, crossing Denbigh Street, we could see the twin chimneys of Battersea power station belching their thick black smoke, the shadows scudding along the swollen Thames. So tired now, for we had not slept for days, livid in shirts and dresses. And Alex's legs had begun to give in, she seemed to somersault across the puddles with this last effort for a stranger's home. My legs felt lightweight. Still, we made it to the notorious house and climbed the stairs that seemed to lead off to the top of the sky. A key had been left for us. And I dropped it many a time, she watching with a glazed, distant look till I pulled the blinds down and sank into a man's wasted bed and suddenly the blessed sickness came on Alex, she bit into my arm, screaming into the old laundered bed, close friends knocked on the hastily-built walls.

Then, when the fit passed, she made me promise never to let her go because she knew that was what I wanted to hear. Now, back in normality, no dreams come, the future separates us.

Reprieve

THEY TOOK a taxi out of Birmingham to their modest lodgings. She sat so silent, it seemed her mind had slipped from her. Peter paid the driver handsomely. Then he argued with her in the room. "There is still time to go back on this," he repeated. She held her silence. She undressed and got carefully into bed. He kept talking away, fretting, worrying her. At this last moment he had ceased being the most generous man in the world.

Yesterday she had had the final consultation with the doctor. "It seems," he said, "that you have your mind made up." Sheila said: "I have." "I see no reason then for any delay," he replied. She had got up and crossed to the door, counting every step, trying to appear a confident, mature strong woman. She must, she had thought, show him. At the door she fainted. She blamed the heat in the room. She said, "Don't take this for weakness or anything like that." The doctor nodded.

Tonight, this man here, her confidant and financial adviser and lover, was having his moral fidgetings. At long last it came, what had been building up in her all night. From the first anxious strain at her heart muscles, from all the days moving between the cottage and the town, now it would happen. The tears burst out, oh just burst out of her eyes, streamed away from her. They came from her loins and wrists, happy life-giving tears and, God, it took the agony out of the room. He tried holding her, thinking his advice had won her. She let him. Then, as the crying subsided, she said, "Look what you're doing! Your boots, ruining the white bedspread!" That his untidiness should strike her just then was unbelievable. To have cared for a strange bedspread in a strange house where she would only spend two nights! But why should he lie there, turning his boots into the bedspread, talking so manfully of choices and life and marriage?

Morning, he dropped her off at the hospital. She was the youngest in the ward. Most were married women of about forty

51

who didn't want any more children. A doctor came and gave her a spectacular shot in the arm. He said, "This will relax you!" There were an awful lot of women being pushed to and fro, and she among them, in wheelchairs. You waited about in wheelchairs for your turn. They chatted there in the corridor, high as sparrows on the morphine.

At last, it was after a day, she was pushed in on a trolley to an amazing place she had never been before. There was the great light-orchestration of the operating theatre, and the doctors in their green outfits moving about talking quietly.

"I want to tell you something, doctor," she said. "You're awful nice, but that injection you gave me. It was very good. But, you see I'm mad awake!" She laughed and laughed. "What has you so happy?" he asked, filling a new syringe, so thin and fine against the round tubular lighting. Of course, all she looked at was his eyes to see if he was a man or a boy. She couldn't tell him, but the flesh between her elbows and shoulders flushed with giddiness and happiness. They pulled back her single white covering. "I hope," she said, as he again lightly tipped the pinprick into the crook of her arm, "that this one works."

Kelly

WHEN HE AWOKE Diane softened the wax in his ear with a kiss. He dressed in the wardrobe, with the door open and the mirror closed. The child was humming softly to himself like a violin searching for a mood. Later, Darcy edged away from everyone to write his diary.

> *March 3rd*
> *I have lived with faith yet never found its expiation. If I have discovered anything it is that life is bare and vital, embroidered by language and laughter, and still so quick that no image can satisfy or symbol call up all the longings. I am at least free of associations. Names have fallen away. The village people have become like shadows, like stains years old. Stains not of blood, for those are the city people walking the streets, alive and caricatured, but the village shadows are old friends, like decaying domestic matter.*
> *It is said that in the shadows hearts beat like the cheers of children greet someone emerging from an underground station, the sudden stinging of sunlight and sky. . .*
> *Enough.*
> *Enough.*

The previous year had been composed of two sounds for Darcy, lake-sound and city-sound, and as time passed the shadows merged but did not strengthen into something articulate and real. The birth of the baby had come with its attendant joys, but was forgotten with the same mediocrity with which his own birth was shelved, allowed slip into his subconscious to snap at him in conventional dreams, as if that reality counted for little. Alternatives and distinctions he found hard to make. His diaries, he felt, were full of a weak-minded subservience to emotional decay. Yet the blurred outlines of life provided a form of hapiness. Off Shaftesbury Avenue, one night a week, he spent at the roulette tables playing the same number, red five. Friday and Saturday, Diane and himself and the child travelled to the races. He loved the sight of a two-year-old running into form and the fall of the chips on the green velvet tables. The roulette wheel became smaller as he won. His bets at the races were small, even if they disturbed the rations in his pocket, they hardly exacted any tribute from his soul. By day Darcy slept in the parks, bought newspapers which he read deeply, setting up for himself the panorama of the world with what perspectives he could conjure, but as he limited himself to reviews and features even his reading became a boring ritual, second-hand. Speeding on Sundays till his jaw locked, he never questioned the matter any further but lay back listening to his two sounds as they developed into shreds. Litter of all kinds filled the streets he walked in at night. In the vegetable markets the drunks sat by their steaming fires, eating bananas and tomatoes and the frosted leaves of cabbages till they curled up for the night by their dead fires, bottles upright or fallen beside them.

That night he waited at an Italian café off Wardour Street for the quarter-full bottles of lager the waiters left out with the rubbish. A glass could only take three-quarters. Here, on the hour, a stiff political drunk used to go. A coloured girl inside the café sniggered when she saw the two men. They sat on a step outside a Chinese supermarket and shared the bottles.

"This is your street?" Darcy asked.

"Yes. You could ask the police," the Pole told him.

They drank some more. The drunk poured his lager through his handkerchief into a paper cup.

"Perhaps I'm drinking your stuff?"

"In this country it does not matter," the older man nodded and together they squatted under the brightly-lit windows filled with white frozen fish and rice alcohol. Darcy knew that the Pole talked politics because he had heard him denouncing the crew that slept at Bishops Gate and when a Scotsman had threatened him, the Pole had wrenched a burning ember from the fire and whirled it. The argument had gone on all night with the rest shouting obscenities out of their sleep, though the two antagonists had seemingly parted without injury at dawn. Darcy asked the Pole about the night in question, but the man never answered. They broke cigarettes and rolled them in Trafalgar Square where they watched a film crew taking down their lights above the fountain. They shared names,

Darcy being pronounced with a long "s" sound that the prayer people use in church for the whispered name of the recurring Jesus. The Pole shortened his name to Kelly. Kelly on this occasion was the dominant, cheerful personality. And Darcy felt a kinship based on a sense of turning from the righteous to the disendowed. Gaining enthusiasm he tried to bring up the older man's philosophy of socialism, but the Pole maintained, "It's firm promise we want, not utopia laced with vodka. Being a pauper does not make me a socialist, you know."

"I did not mean that."

"Do not use me as a ploy for criticism. Perhaps your individual ignorance will blind you."

But Kelly knew the merits of London, he named buildings and their owners with malice and confidence, as if the world were the size of a two-penny piece. His English was perfect except when he was aroused and then the verbs were half-checked by a foreign emotion. Darcy explained about the two sounds that troubled him and Kelly took his time until the whole matter was explained and then he, too, said he remembered fields and suchlike, but it was a long time ago. The industry, the material of the world mattered as much to him now.

"I was a railway man and then a teacher. Even still I listen for whistles in my sleep, feel comfortable when a train passes. I like the railway yards, building sites, the sounds of a building growing, everything that I find half-buried in the ground that a man made, that he made to make something else."

"Do you mean archaeology?"

"No. No, I do not mean archaeology."

And then he asked Darcy for exact pictures of his heart's place, and nodded and nodded and questioned again.

After changing their minds many times they reached Kelly's house in a derelict row near Battersea. Her jaw was swollen out like a red head of lettuce and her upper teeth hung down threatening to pierce the awful, permanent swelling. She was drinking tea by the window when they entered. The Pole took off his coats and shirts immediately. He hung his socks out on the window-ledge. Pigeons walked on a ledge opposite with their chests puffed out. They were seven stories up in a grey-bricked smoky morning and the tea was strong that the Yorkshire woman made. Lucy was her name. Despite her condition, her internal sympathies had not stopped — they had deepened. More tea was made. She spread the table again after cleaning up every crumb. Every few minutes another cigarette. Endless journeys into her bag. Time was compassionate yet irrational, what with the everyday complexity of news she used to read. All of four or five popular papers. Darcy had often seen her speaking to the Pole in the Labour Exchange in Victoria, carrying her six Woolworth's bags of odds and ends that she sorted out and arranged as she waited for her money. The officials treated her with humanity perhaps because she was an easy case to identify, checking her bags constantly for nuances, for relief. Kelly made soup from leeks and onions he had collected in the market, adding chunks of potatoes and carrots. Lucy cut bread and then read out the sporting pages of the *Evening News*, naming each horse that was running with a quiet, humorous wonder.

"Dark Sky, Wephen, Venus of Streatham," she said.

"No two horses, dears, with the one name," she said.

They slept on two sofas while she slept in a double bed the Pole had taken from downstairs when they'd broken in. Everything had been hauled upstairs, paintings, plants, old shirts, a breakfast cooker, Sunday magazines. The local social workers had come around to help them. Lucy laughed when they were mentioned, saying how sometimes they came up here and smoked dope and once Kelly had unwittingly left them in fits of laughter when he described the night he had been knocked over by a car, left for dead and come to soaked by a cloud-burst.

"The radical intelligentsia drive such cars," Kelly muttered at the end of her story.

They talked about Darcy's family from their various beds. "I'd like to have had a child," Lucy said, becoming serious, as if she had just realized it for the first time. But later Darcy was to discover that this was her way, each act of faith, of belief, even of memory, had to be relived time and time again, each gesture reaffirmed.

As they bedded down the metropolis was coming alive. The guilty were innocent again. "It's the creation of the artefact rather than its use enthralls me," whispered Kelly, "the will of the people to act in a certain direction." There was silence while Kelly collected his thoughts. "But sometimes socialism gained in theory through the competitiveness of its masters, rather than out of concern for humanity." He nodded, turned and slept. And the two sounds came back to Darcy. He wrote in the silence.

March 4th
For the first time I understand that real tragedy is the sudden vision of unceasing humanity, unceasing nature. It could even be personal. It could even be optimistic. This man Kelly is very funny. An emaciated walk and a dry smile. Half the time he spends making up proverbs. If I remember properly, he said earlier: "The making of things is not a function of the things themselves but of the people who make them". He does not like the Irish. "One does not seek one's likenesses," he says. He says, "Where the working class is divided, where one half is nationalistic and religiously different from the other, then those that fight on either side are predominantly fascist. The Irish will not grow up. They want to be loved or feared, yet they will surrender their country eventually into the hands of the bourgeoisie." He makes it sound very easy and fatalistic and as if politics were to be taken seriously. Politics are shit. Don't I know.

The Pole slept with his eyes open and often the other man thought Kelly was looking at him even in his dreams and his stomach turned with fear at the paleness, lifelessness of the sleeping expatriate and before morning had passed he crept over on his hands and knees, first closed one lid, waited a while then shut the other, and after he crept back and fell asleep he was unaware that the older man's mouth had fallen open.

Darcy was crossing St James's Park the following afternoon to see his young wife. He was making sure that they would not argue, knowing that confrontations usually resolve in new patterns of uneasy co-existence. In a way, he knew his plight did not matter. The day was warm and everyone was relaxed. But inside him his mind hungered for politics, like all guilty emigrants. *How hastily drawn the mind is*, he wrote down below his piece of the night before, *How sober its sketches*. What he shared with his wife was a quiet desperation that no fantasy could sustain. He walked past Anne's Court, down Victoria Street, up Rochester Row past the military and police barracks, across Tatchbrook Street market and all the time he was thinking, repeating, stopping. It was getting darker and little lights caught the white-coated girls and straw-hatted men under the small stalls. Corsetry, wools, haberdashery. Seedless sultanas and green grapes. Shellfish and scampi. Delph sets, light blue and green with castles and small churches painted on them. Viennese whirls, chocolate delights and cherry delights. Tripe. Past the Duchess of Clarence.

Spanish voices mixed with English.

The cats of Pimlico were abroad among the vegetables and a kitten he had befriended once he saw slip, hold on to her step, as she walked a roof ledge four stories up. It seemed a shame that he could so easily identify with a kitten when there were a thousand human ghosts in whose limbs he could climb dangerously, look from their eyes, feel their hunger.

"Welcome home stranger," said Diane. She left him and the child together while she went shopping. The boy was dreaming a bit, letting little murmurs that she said resembled the "sky-goat", after the sounds of a snipe's wing. And it was just that sound, a sudden flurry from the side of a marsh, a bird-scuffle. She had that knack of naming those far-away sounds, not romantically, but exactly, finding their complement among their lives and it was her clear eye sometimes he envied. He stole from her secret place under the carpet a pound, and lifted up the child who had nearly begun to cry. They hung together in the room.

"Dadedadedada," he sang to his son.

"A measure of figs and barley," he sang.

The child looked up and frowned, he nearly had a personality his father could recognize. He pulled at his clothes and at his ear. Was what the child saw something of warmth, something of decay, a face that he might never focus on, that might never emerge from the half-light. The man saw the distance between himself and the child. The child like his wife was learning to live with a hypocrite, he thought, and then they moved together again and the boy murmured ah. . . aho. . . ahoahaoahaooahhahoooooahahahah-ahahao. . . ah. He whirled his fists in the air and smiled. And frowned. The room was impeccable. Darcy lay on the bed with his son on his chest and felt for a few moments the warmth of lying in his own place. Diane had a new plant marked thistledown on the chest of drawers. The place had been like a discarded planet when they had moved in but now she was gaining confidence, they had cleared a bathroom, broke into a drawing-room. When he stayed too much at home he shared his inertia, but while he stopped away things got done, the child grew.

When he kissed the child, he kissed his wife. The dishonesty lay on his side because he harboured thwarted ambitions. Arguments abounded, as if too long had been spent in interpretation without the satisfaction of creation. Or it might have been because he loved both equally, that himself and Diane transferred all their nervous energy through the child, Lester.

Lester was a vehicle for their fear.

But the child, when he smiled, refuted all this.

"I can imagine a time," said Diane when she returned, "when the two of you will be enemies of mine."

His son had fallen asleep across his chest and Darcy lifted him, his head hanging lifeless, into the Victorian cot. "He is like a postage stamp there among his blankets," Diane remarked. Tiny pebbles of milk dotted the child's lips and Darcy wiped them away before heading down into the street, intense with afternoon sound, as if structure and movement had locked in an anticlimax.

He read what he'd written down of Kelly's words. "Everything at work in the factory complies with some known law of the outside world, and was in existence previously in Nature and in harmony with it. This, socialism would preserve."

The Pole was on his hunkers in the Dole. He was rocking gently on his soles. Darcy saw him through the window. They did not greet each other. It was as if the Pole did not recognize him. The queue reached out into the street, a mixture of actors and actresses, the drunks and the poor. An hour passed before he reached the inside of the office. Late spring rain began to fall and the perplexed sleepers on the pavement and doorsteps awoke and stumbled off into the park next to Scotland Yard to find cover beneath the trees. Kelly was claiming that the Exchange was stealing money from him. "Yes, you," he shouted across the counter, his fists tight against his thighs. "You steal my money, you bastard." The official withdrew with a smile. Darcy cashed his giro in the post office and won an easy twenty pounds in the bookies. He walked at the crowds, loving the sense of flow, the endless human silence. Again. The Pole was arguing with two policemen outside Scotland Yard. He could even have been asking them to arrest the official in the Dole. A young policeman was taking the argument seriously, much to the chagrin of his older companion. The young policeman shook his arms trying to restrain the argument of the stiff, small foreigner, who would walk off, return, and start all over, till the policeman turned eventually to a baffled American who was looking for directions.

Kelly strode angrily off into the rain.

Darcy followed at a safe distance behind him through the park. Kelly interrogated passers-by over simple things, leaving the complex alone. Kelly mad knew much more than Kelly sane. Darcy prepared what he would say to him when they met, but at each approach he faltered. What he meant to say became a ridiculous rhyme in his mind. Eventually, in the Mall, they met and the Pole was genuinely happy. They embraced a long time. They drank Valpolicella in the park. Throughout the summer. Sometimes the cold wet bit into their hands. Till eventually, gardeners, with their arses in the air weeded and rooted in the flowerbeds, while tractors circled, following the piles of leaves that were fed into cages drawn behind.

"What did I think?" Kelly was saying. "It's so. We had a great empire and were ready for dictatorship but other countries were quicker. Our revolution happened elsewhere, among our enemies. Our sense of Nationalism never happened so that Internationalism might follow."

"Then Ireland has a chance?"

"No. No chance at all."

Still, their friendship was sealed. And so began the process of learning for Darcy, a mixture of ambiguity and anger, the loss of guilt, a trimming of personal ambition. They moved about the city throughout the following months, picking up a day's work washing or serving in cafés on the Serpentine or hotels in Knightsbridge, sometimes arguing, sometimes drinking in silence. When Franco died they read the Spanish poets, when the rains came they sat up in the bandstand in St James's Park conducting an imaginary choir, they butressed the ends of sidewalks with a gang from Mayo, served food at a wedding in Brixton, and by the end of the winter Angola had risen, Rhodesia was beginning to tremble and Solzhenitsyn had visited England, complete with the laurels of Western policy. The workers' marches had begun earnestly in England and Russia had again taken its historical place as the threat in Europe, and looking back a hundred years on, as we look back a hundred years to slums and hunger, the historian will see how the slums have moved to the Third World out of harm's way, how hunger and recrimination increaseth. And at the mention of Stalin Kelly would break out into his own language with a merciless tirade. And Northern Ireland people died under the same circumstances.

The pattern was complete.

And in November Darcy burnt his hand at a fireworks display.

December 2nd
Myself and Kelly got work today cleaning a number of Odeon cinemas. It means we will see four different films in a fortnight. With the money we will eat well at Christmas.

Sometimes Diane and the child accompanied the two men on their trips, as did Lucy. When the two women met for the first time it had proved frightening. It was the night himself and the Pole got drunk in Piccadilly and had arrived back to his wife's squat in the small hours, dragging Lucy reluctantly along. His wife was asleep when they arrived. They tiptoed about the room. Kelly kissed the child repeatedly, amazed by the sudden surprised looks, Lester blinking in the sudden light at night, the hand thrown, the legs askew, watching the stranger till the end with the contemplation of a child. When Diane awoke and saw the Yorkshire woman sipping Guinness at the bottom of her bed, she buried her head beneath the blankets. When she had properly woken, they were reconciled and Kelly gave a long and garbled speech. And after Lucy had fallen asleep, Kelly stood a long time in the moonlight looking down on the ruins each side of them, talking quietly to himself, as if he underestimated Darcy, and then he lay down while they turned over their good luck in their minds.

But over the months Darcy succeeded in owing a lot of money. And though everyone disapproved, still he gambled at roulette and racing, and his debts grew larger. It was something crept up on him. His notes and diaries remained untouched and now his dreams were of winning, of breaking even, of leaving gambling aside. But each morning his nerves resolved and the game began again in earnest. Diane cooked extraordinary meals each evening and they prepared to go down in style, Kelly, Lucy and themselves. Each took turns to feed the child. And each imagined fearful diseases they could catch from each other and everyone feared for the child because he suspected no one, but thrived among the crowds in the kitchen.

Through time the lakes and fields that once existed were forgotten, the park, a peremptory pause between buildings, as Darcy moved from tension into conflict.

It took only meeting a distraught Kelly in the park to defuse Darcy's enthusiasm. The older man's nose was running, but he had an answer, "Everyone thinks they see my weak side opposed to my strong side, against my will, in fact it is with my will, my whole being spurs me on."

The last day they spent in the park the air was hard and sharp, the water covered by a white cloud of seagulls and among them the green head of a duck, the black compact body of a waterhen. The unlit lights over the bridge hung down in the fading daylight like blue leaves. Yet in the sombre unreal air Darcy was full of a tremendous enthusiasm, his heart sang. Now that he had nothing he had allayed his sins, the poor were his family. At first he had only dimly understood, but now the old selfish haunts of his psyche had been exorcized and his despair was no longer self-perpetuating. Darcy's need to understand and the need to contribute may have been what depressed Kelly, but Darcy continued, "Of course I have doubts." He saw that this new political consciousness gave a certain security, especially in London, that could not be tested. He was begging Kelly for praise. For theirs was a type of intimacy not easily entered into, a sarcasm that severed Darcy from his old personal wounds yet frightened the vanity of his individual soul. But his old comrade was drunk. "I'm not quite the happier emerging communal spirit today," he said. Darcy was aware of the drumming of veins across the back of his comrade's hands. Over the past few weeks Kelly's drinking had increased, he had been growing impatient and this afternoon's walk was shorter and tenser than ever before.

It was as if they suspected each other of insincerity, as if their companionship had been merely neutral and intellectual.

For the first time Darcy found himself alone and his mind was blank.

"We could travel," Diane said. "It's time for travelling."

"We have no money. The child's too young."

"What's wrong with you is you're bored. When people are bored they are destructive. You could go off by yourself."

But the thought of travelling alone frightened him.

The following day the Pole disappeared and nothing was heard of him for a fortnight. Darcy searched the streets by night and the Yorkshire woman joined him one fearsome winter's night when the heavens had burst. The rain dampened and opened one of her bags so that all those treasured papers spilled in a line behind them, as if to say that things would never be the same again. A couple of weeks later he received a note from Kelly.

> Dear fellow Catholic,
> I am recuperating here. The drama of the people is every-where. Each day I think of the turning of matter into an element and its history is like a great poem. We are like earth, water, air, fire. My body is not so quick so I shall take my time here. It is warm and comfortable and my brother's pills keep me amused. Give my love to Diane and Lester.
> Yours, J. Kowaleski
> PS You probably expected me to be in a madhouse — that would suit your romanticism.

Darcy immediately crossed London to the suburbs where Kelly's brother kept a transport café. He bought a coffee and sat down among the lorry drivers and security men. They talked horses. After his third coffee he asked for Kelly. The woman directed him to a hospital that lay up the road from the café, set in its own elaborate grounds. It was not grey like city hospitals, but newly painted with yellow and green and surrounded by intricate shrubbery and cane plants and gravel paths that led hither and thither across the lawns. His enthusiasm forbade him to think, for would they not embrace each other as of old. In the foyer he imagined he heard the cry of the "sky-goat". A nurse explained that Mr Kowaleski was a day patient and was out walking. Minutes later Kelly was led into the clinical-smelling waiting-room and they embraced. They walked out onto a broad glass-covered terrace where patients in pyjamas and nightgowns were talking and looking down the lawns, complaining softly to each other with terrible intimacy.

The heat in the enclosure was intense, although outside it had already begun to snow.

"Look," said his comrade, "I am lucky. And behind that hill there is a library and down that path a pond."

But Darcy was shocked by the mad lifeless gleam in the Pole's eyes. It reminded him of the night his eyes had remained open while he slept, like cracks that opened to nowhere. Death was closer here than on a battlefield, yet Kelly cajoled and talked and joked. When he coughed at his own mirth he turned away. Through the hospital seemed to flow all the treason, all the tragedy that man could encompass. "This is my friend Darcy," he said, imitating his Irish accent and the patients shook hands with him. "To the nurses here I am a healthy man so you must say nothing," he whispered as they left for the café. "I like to laugh and talk with them and give no cause for fear." They drank two glasses of wine with his brother, who never spoke but looked continually at the ground as Kelly joked with him, and later Darcy left for town, drinking all the way, and arrived home, dead drunk.

April 5th
Kelly is not mad, he is just invulnerable. His apparent sickness has left me with a long way to go. The distance frightens me. I am aware how I clung to him when he wanted me to let go. It was to guard myself. Now I am aware of this disorder, I can become an equal and a friend. Next I must free Diane. The absence of a god makes my heart lighter.

When the next note arrived from Kelly a few days later he put off the moment of reading it till he arrived under the great wall of scaffolding that cramped St James's Park underground station. Warmth came up from under the footpath. He was sad knowing purity was impossible. And was purity important anyway? Was purity not a lack of knowledge or non-acceptance of change and growth? What was important was the encountering of demands greater than one's limitations. A sense of purpose. But what saddened him most was the personal defence mechanism that destroyed a relationship so newly born.

Above him the traditional Greek music of building went on. First a hammer sounded, an engine roared and these were answered by a gong inside the building, a crane swung by in silence, huge buckets opened with a crash into a dumper, pigeons flew by in silence, a yell, taut wires screamed and hauled a load of concrete overhead while he sat watching, gazing, and painters inside were painting the wall's a deep office grey, while the great sheets of cellophane that covered the building tossed in the wind, flapping like a soul trapped by temporary materials.

At last he opened the letter.

Dear fellow Catholic,
This Christmas five years ago my neighbours were gunned down in the shipyards of Gydnia. I pray for them now. What I hate most is how the young live off the old, it drains me of strength. How they make images and likenesses of themselves. Watch now for the blackbirds in the park for this is their time of year. We are timeless. In Poznan in 1956 the workers hung the militia men from the lamp-posts, lynched them, or in Gydnia flung them into the sea. It will happen all over again. All the things I have told you can be found in our literature. I have no drink for three days. I am sick but not dying and perhaps will see you again on my return. Give my love to Lester and Diane.
   Yours, J. Kowaleski
PS I dream continually of women.

Betrayal

THIS MAN and woman, he in his late thirties and she in her early twenties were lying behind a tuft of thistles and weeds, a small raised place, alongside the river. They lay away from the village towards the lake. Water-hens moved quickly from them as they kissed and went out of sight by the reeds, and then appeared again, moments later, swimming easily without haste. The man was coughing and the woman was kissing his chest. When he turned on his back there was sky, so abnormally huge and filled with colossal movement of blue and white that no vertical could last there but must burn itself out before a straight line could ever be righted. She and then he, changing position, looked into the earth. Hoof-print and daisy. She accepted the burning thistles at her back. He looked around once in fear of being seen.

This man and woman were driving aimlessly along until they came to a village. He took her around. She was perfectly natural and quiet among the people. In the house of the postmistress she talked little which attracted attention. He wondered, as the son of the house spoke with nostalgia of the past, how much he loved her? For surely he must love her? He had no need to invent anything to protract their time together, the truth became like the act of imagination, reaching right out of their lives, till only what mattered was separated. What they bridged flowed freely beneath them — it was great for him to be with such a person. He took her down a river he knew. First to show her the separation of the two lakes under the eighteenth-century bridge. On one side brown trout were kept from coarse fish on the other. Now the dangerous dam was outdated, yet still held the two powerful waters from each other. The second lake had since been cleared for trout, but in the deep waters the coarse fish still persisted. Trout now danced on both sides. The couple kept walking out to the mouth. Not a long journey, sufficient to point out all that happened as a child, cows eating swimmers' clothes and the coldness of river water. They lay away from the village that they might not be seen. Ducks fled them. A pike ran out of the new, deep, muddy water by the reeds.

This man and woman talked of their worries. Then they stopped talking because of the indulgence and the emptiness. They were not drawn to this place. The act of walking together, bit by bit, brought them closer to a small slight place in time. A fearful human place. Their situation, outside of these few moments together, appeared impossible. She slipped into mud hastening in the wrong path after him, just like a trusting young girl. The entire river was filled with the smell of new-mown hay; no trees sheltered the path and approaching the mouth a dry cold wind blew in over desolate bad land. They lay in the ugliest place. They felt each other not with abandon or passion or discovery, but slowly, fearfully, treasuring. Neither did they make love, for the inner tissues of her vagina would cling coldly to his weak penetration. Nor could they satisfy their need of being swept away, from the dam and the separation, to the mouth and the open sky. But kissed and held each other gratefully, and returned singly, though they would have loved to hold hands throughout this village, along the banks, amidst the people.

This man and woman were bound and exposed to others. The man was coughing and the woman kissed his chest. He kissed her childless breasts. They looked down to the blonde lip of the vagina, the thin red lip of the penis. Desire passed through their hands, each to the other. Yet nothing happened and nothing drove them away. He was impatient and she was eager. She was waiting on him in a traditional manner, till he might break with his responsibilities, as he before in a previous but continuous life, with a different woman, had broken with other social decrees. Hurrying, she said he would stop as he was. And he thought he would leave, but going meant leaving everyone, even her.

He satisfied himself this way, and would not be betrayed.

Love

HER HOUSE was a half-hour's walk away, time when anything might happen, up one of the many steep hills at that side of the city.

As he climbed, forgetting places the minute he passed them, he arrived at one house with bright lights on in the living-room. Books were piled on pine shelves from ceiling to floor and a newly varnished table sat in the middle of the room. The room was empty. Whoever they were, they didn't care except for cleanliness. But a few streets away someone was playing a record loud enough for him or her to own their own house. That was marvellous too. To be able to cross your own floor without fear of tomorrow. The houses were modern, each piled lower than the next, with little lawns, and sometimes two cars in the driveway, parked hurriedly, and odd times a motorcycle, the front wheel swung sideways and the pillion gleaming with dew.

Also in many of the rooms people were reading upside down.

The rooms had that look, the blinds drawn half-way and the light low enough to be beside the bed, the atmosphere concentrated as the reader pored over the pages and his shadow drifted across the ceiling like something constant, so that he might be living anywhere in the world, looking back on himself from above.

He stood in the gateway opposite the house and looked up at her window.

Soon, he sat up on the pier, enjoying the sensation of leaving the pull of the earth behind, and he began to coax her out of bed, into her clothes, through the thin bedroom door, down the stairs quietly.

He looked at the door, willing it to open.

The door did not open.

But the old house swayed on its foundations like a single man drunk in a crowd of men desiring a woman. It swayed like that a long time and would not settle.

Next, he stood on the pier, gently balanced there, as if he might reach the same level as herself.

He thought of her, warm and comfortable among the dry sheets, looking at the ceiling, waiting on her house to grow still. Just now she would be slipping out of the heavy cotton nightdress that came to her ankles. Searching in the dark for a clean pair of knickers. Pulling them over her warm cheeks so that they nestled around her groin like a soft loving hand. The skin stretched between her shoulder blades. Next, she pulled the knitted dress over her head and tugged it down about her back, swivelling her hips till it fitted. The boots and the white socks. Looks behind her, taking along her brother's oilskin coat and, maybe, a flower-patterned toilet bag. Across the landing, her father stirs in his sleep on the sitting-room couch. She approaches the door on tiptoe. Jimmy waited anxiously.

But the door did not open.

The street remained quiet. Nothing moved. He walked up and down.

The night swelled up like something about to burst and as day descended he confused the contours of the window and the door, then the house became the same as the others in its terrace as the sun branded the new day on the loose curtains.

Finally he ran down the hill at half-five, past the solitary workers climbing from the poorer areas below in their donkey jackets, with innocent, bad-tempered faces. The cleaning ladies letting themselves into the insurance offices turned to look out through the glass doors before they began their work, as if obliged to go over the paths that took them there. But their leader, who was deaf and dumb, had already begun; she lashed out at the first step, while her laughing conversation with herself echoed all the way up to the seventh floor, returning like a tribal memory. He caught his breath outside his home and went in, sure of his terrible crime, and yet he went on counting until he had reached a figure that would redeem him. The bed was so cold that it seemed like a deserted ship in which monkeys travelled, but lying there he did not feel misery or loneliness, but planned ahead for the next time, telling himself that tomorrow night she must come.

Frank kept shouting from the street below, "Come on, mate, get up," his hand pressed to the horn. The boy sat into the Transit and said nothing as the remorseless drive through the caged roadways began. "Are we in love?" Frank asked, laughing. "Leave it out," said Jimmy. "Nothing I like better than driving straight at the bastards," said Frank. Once they started working Jimmy was not too bad, for his enthusiasms multiplied without his knowing, but after a dinner of chops and mushrooms in the transport café, he stretched out his legs so that they were filled with warm tired blood and he fell asleep with a grown-up sigh in the green, wooden chair. "Bloody hell," he heard Frank saying, "are you off again?" "I'm not sleeping," said Jimmy, irritated, without opening his eyes, "I was just thinking, like." "Oh yeh," replied Frank, who then, finding something suspicious in the eyes of a lorry driver at the next table, forgot all about Jimmy, turned aside and sang along with a record he hardly knew.

Somehow or another Jimmy got through the day.

But they had problems, Frank and his apprentice.

For while the timber was prised along the levels of the old walls, the spirit level continually called for more adjustment and as they hauled the hardboard onto the roof, they left behind them a trail of asbestos slates that must be mended. He kept Jimmy at it so that they could finish early, and gave him the easy jobs, like stacking the unused wallboard under the rainproof sheets in the valley of the club house where he could look over the tennis courts, cricket fields and bowling greens to Highgate Hill, and each time he looked he turned to Frank and the two would stop working.

"It's weird, isn't it?" Jimmy would ask.

"What's that?"

"I'll go up there and she mightn't come the next time either."

"I hope for your sake she does," then Frank dropped the lead soundlessly onto the path, looked at it and said: "A man is always exaggerating what he don't know."

They resumed work and Frank skated along the ledge, his hammer hopping off his thigh and his hands searching, like a stall lady's, in his leather apron for the proper pins.

Strange thoughts on the edge of sleep entered Jimmy's head as he waited in his room. Sometimes he found himself speaking across to Frank in his dead father's language. Though Frank was twice his age, in this fantasy they were equals in age and experience, so Jimmy had no fear of telling the truth and Frank, for his part, was devoting a lot of time to listening to Jimmy, who was telling him a way out of certain difficulties, same as they might be seeking to seal a joint or to find the best way to let the tension in their planks carry a dead weight of material away and beyond what appeared possible.

In this talk a great deal of responsibility rested easily on Jimmy's shoulders, and when he realized himself again, he would have dearly loved to talk, talk yards, for Frank was reluctant to leave go of him.

Eventually though he put on his corduroys and a T-shirt that didn't fit him.

He fondled the pay packet in his pocket, saying, I have control again.

This time he took his torch and, because of the message instilled in him by the imaginary conversation with Frank, he stopped outside his mother's door. She was snoring in a faraway lonely fashion, troubled by the hot night, sounding as if she had fallen asleep too suddenly to retain any of her memories. Her door gave way to his touch, and he looked carefully in to see that the single sheet had slipped off with her continuous turning. Her breasts and groin were like those of another, younger woman who took her place when night fell.

He withdrew quietly, like an intruder, put the torch in his knapsack and slipped out into the street. Tonight the streets were more alive, the Indian shops smelt of cardamom and the supermarkets of hosed-down floors and every so often he met groups of three or four people ghosting along, very sure of themselves, as if there was great safety in numbers.

"Rassholes," he whispered to himself.

At the bottom of the hill, he passed a house where a party was still on.

Here the woodwork was aged and slanted and the house itself seemed to tilt towards the road because of the hundreds of plants on the off-angle sills. He waited to see would anything happen, but the room where the repetitive music was playing was in darkness, except for the thin glow of joints, and in the room above the party a woman passed over and back with a baby at her shoulder, and he

waited until the woman had found relief for the child, losing himself for the first few minutes of another's distress, then he went up
the wandering footpath, under the little bridges, through the
tunnels, up the rows of steps till behind him the lights went around
the face of the city, lighting up what was immediately beneath their
steaming lamps.

He looked back to see how far he had come and it wasn't far.

He looked especially along the houses each side of him, but this
part of the hill was dark.

It was only the old and retired lived here.

You could tell by the broken gates and the absence of cars, and
by the care given to the vegetables growing in neat lines, onions
and cabbages, where elsewhere there were easy lawns. By the
windows, heavily protected with curtains, the gnomes nestled in
the overgrown shrubbery. And sometimes a face appeared at a
window that may or may not have been there, cringing at the
stupidity of the mysteries left from the universe they started with,
just a second ago.

The moon was held by a firm hand over the village. He looked up
with a catch in his throat. The white curtains were pulled in her
room, but next door, in her brother's room, the light was on. This
was it, Jimmy said to himself. She is waiting on him to go to sleep.
He sat on the wall opposite laughing to himself. I've made it, he
said, shaking his head. He never took his eyes off her brother's
window. He could tell by the sense of the room that people were up
there walking around, but now he wished tiredness on them, it was
half-four in the morning. The light went out. Then the front door
was opening. He jumped over the wall, stretched out on the grass
and waited, the pulse beating in his wrist like a cyclist's foot.
Someone shouted goodnight, then footsteps crossed over to where
he was. He hugged the wall. The steps continued alongside where
he lay and went down the hill. He looked up. The house was in
darkness. Now, he thought.

He gave three sharp bursts of the torch.

Waited.

Searched the windows and the door. Again. Nothing. He shone
the torch into his face for a full five minutes, throwing all caution

to the wind, expecting at any minute some strange hand to descend on his shoulder. He switched the torch on full and turned his face upwards to her window, so that his features became distorted and appeared like those of an old man, who, starting with his eyes, was slowly becoming transparent. When he switched off the torch he could see nothing for ages, but heard only his own voice reciting numbers in a nightmarish fashion.

The street was spinning away from him.

He rubbed his eyes in panic, but when his normal sight returned, her house was as it had always been and now, earlier than last night, becoming part of the terrace again. The morning traffic started to thunder into the city limits and stray voices shouted from room to room their indifference to the watcher in the street below.

For the first time he dreaded failure.

That he might take the easy way out. Let all these objects pile up to infinity so that he might have no power over them.

He saw nor heard anything on the descent. The street off the Holloway Road was scattered with debris from the night before. The skips full of rubbish and the leavings of parties. Not without caution he entered the house, then darted under the stairs when he heard someone moving above. His mother was talking to his sister. "Where is he?" she was saying. "What?" asked his sister in a sleepy voice. "He's not in his bed, I tell you." Jimmy pulled off his clothes and bundled them out of sight. He tousled his hair, and with a perpetual yawn went up the stairs in his vest and Y-fronts.

His mother was returning from his sister's room when she saw him. "Oh," she said and pulling her housecoat about her disappeared in the recesses of her bedroom, as if nothing had happened.

Jimmy slipped down and brought up his clothes.

And lay a long time looking at himself above, while in their various beds his family found more comfortable positions, sighed and tried to forget about everything. Jimmy tried to drown out the selfish complaints of his sister's boyfriend, who had been woken in the rumpus and wanted to know what was happening. His complaints called up an image of something becoming less than it should be. He did not dislike the man for himself but for the burden he brought to bear on his sister, and Jimmy blamed her for the weakness in not waiting to take someone who would have given her the pleasure she craved. But soon their voices stopped, their complaints became echoes and the boy had the tired morning to himself. That was strange, too, how short the distance to her unfriendly house was becoming. It was nearly as if it were next door, only a wall separating them, if you came down to it. He turned to the wall, his two fists hugging his rib cage and steeled his mind from other things till he could see her cross to the window, you must be doing that now, just now, Oh my Lord, push the curtains aside and search the street for him, yet not see him though he was there, Here, over here, he whispers, then she goes up onto her toes so that the nightdress rises a fraction, looks off to her left, he runs into her line of vision but she looks through him again, then suddenly his mother interrupted from next door, "Go down and pay the girls, James, man dear. Right?" And then, anticipating her dead husband's reply, she continued in a soft sympathetic manner, "Ah, but they are worth it, James, they are worth it," and, greatly pleased that he was back again, she lifted him up like an infant into her arms.

Jimmy woke with a heavy headache from hunger and a sense of having slept through many crises. The house was empty. They were at the sale-of-work in the church opposite looking for bargains. The TV was on. The pot of stew simmered away, its grey fat having come to the surface with bubbles of paprika and parsley. He peeled the bag of sweet blue potatoes and left them ready in a bowl of water. Ate some Weetabix and treacle. Looked around the hot, shimmering garden.

He could concentrate on nothing and his heart kept pounding away so that it wasn't easy.

Madge's boyfriend came in.

"You were all in good voice last night, as usual," he lisped.

"I'm sorry," replied Jimmy, speaking for them all, "I can't help it."

"Yeh, we are living in a hen house."

Jimmy sat there hoping Stan would not start on about women, but still he could not bear to leave the kitchen, afraid that what he had might be suddenly taken from him. Stan liked to talk to Jimmy about sex, because the boy would grow perplexed and inferior. He thought he would soon break down the boy's reserve. He wanted to kill that look of fear in the boy's eye, stamp out that stupidity by talking of all the obscenities he could conjure up. But what really drove him to these excesses was Jimmy's untroubled affinity with the women of the house, and the pleasure the boy took in their company, meaning, Stan reckoned, that the boy was dependent, would never know women and maybe grow to hate them.

"Look at them motorcycles go," said Stan.

Then, Madge and her mother came in carrying two pairs of Tesco bags. Madge had got two scarves, a tartan skirt, some old-fashioned bead necklaces and four striped pillow slips. "What do you think, Jimmy?" she asked, holding the skirt to her waist. "It's good," said Jimmy.

"Get out of the light," complained Stan.

"Will you like me in this?" she asked Stan.

"I'd like you," he laughed, "no matter what you were in."

After dinner, Uncle George arrived.

His hair was brilliantined and he was in his finest blue serge. He had that enthusiastic Saturday-night air about him which everybody in the house knew so well, and two library books for his sister-in-law which he slapped on the table, tapped them with his finger and quickly told the story of each, though none could follow him. Stan showed him the new freezer. Uncle George said he had found a place where you could buy meat for bargain prices in Kentish Town, then, "Peggy," he said, before he could be further drawn, "I'll need the lad tonight, the cursed guards are becoming a menace," and before she could reply, he went on about the outrageous cost of the boat back to Ireland, and his remonstrations against public bodies carried such weight that his intrusion into his sister-in-law's private life was forgotten, so that she nodded absent-mindedly and lay back on the cushions of the settee, the way Jimmy loved her to lie, stretched out in a comfortable position from which to view her family, till Uncle George slapped his thighs and kneaded his hands, saying, "We'd best be off," and Madge and Stan saw them to the door in order to see whether the car would start, and for their pleasure Jimmy opened the door to let his gross uncle enter, slammed it shut and walked around the car with a soldier's bearing, then drove off with his right hand raised in a posh farewell.

On the trip to the Feathers, as always, Uncle George found it necessary to turn from his entertaining self into a responsible crank, belittling his sister-in-law for staying behind closed doors. "It can't be good for her, you know," as if going up to the Feathers with him would somehow extend her life, but turning into the carpark, his uncle relaxed from this meaningless tirade, gave Jimmy a wholesome nudge, and said, "Ah, never mind me."

And then, "I'll look after you after." He took the long way round.

When Uncle George was inside drinking, Jimmy sat in the car listening to the radio.

Sometimes on a night they might drive to five pubs, picking up more passengers as they went on, for Uncle George only braved company because he could not drink alone, and the drunken men in the back would praise Jimmy's driving and George's reasoning, a pair who could so well spite the law of the land, and they talked of the barmen as if they were close relations, fathers and mothers to them, the best or the worst in the world, and other brave talk while the nights shortened and their sons grew.

"What more could I ask," Uncle George would happily maintain, "than to have my own chauffeur?"

In the Feathers they were playing tunes that Jimmy could not remember

Outside, somebody stepped it out, enunciating in clear Italian cockney his story from the Bible. "In my house, yes sir, there are many mansions," then the speaker strode along in an easy but determined manner, telling what the Lord says, and encountered without stopping those coming in the opposite direction, his clean boots striking the pavement in a kind of joy, he swung across the street, looked up at the shop fronts to see where he was and went on.

"Right, lad, the Indians," said Uncle George at closing time. He was tilting towards Mecca and accompanied by a blonde woman of about forty, with washy brown skin, whose ailment in her back was now forgotten.

Uncle George stuffed a fiver in Jimmy's lap and kissed him full on the lips. Jimmy drove to the Holloway Road and stopped at the café where the pair bought Ceylon hot mutton curries and cold lagers to take away. Then he drove them to the block of council flats where his uncle had a bachelor flat on the fifth floor.

"It's a roof over my head," Uncle George explained.

"Won't it do you?" she joked.

They did not move for a few moments but sat in silence, looking out each side of them.

"Make sure," his uncle said, banging on the roof of the car, "that you bring her back tomorrow, matey, in one piece."

"Shut it, Georgie," said the woman. She searched in her bag as if its oddments never ceased to surprise her. Then, finding nothing else, she pressed a Mass card for her dead brother into Jimmy's hand. The black, tiny photograph smelt of old perfume. "He was the spit of me," she whispered, as if to find some reason for what she had done. Some people were like that, Jimmy knew. He reversed the car, turned and shot by his uncle who, with a bewildered grin shouted, "Tomorrow," then let go with a long whistle between his finger, thumb and lip that echoed across the concrete playground, then the two stood side by side under the dilapidated floors waiting on the urine-smelling lift to descend.

Madge and Stan were lying on the living-room carpet watching the end of the late night film. The sight of them together looked so false that a feeling of nervous sickness attacked Jimmy's stomach and he sought to escape, with that desperate knowledge that all ways led back here, among relationships he had no place in.

Stan got up and putting his arm around the boy, he led him into the hall.

"Here," he said, taking Jimmy's hand, "go on, further down. "Now that's what's keeping your sister happy".

"That's what you think," answered Jimmy.

"It embarrasses you, doesn't it?"

Jimmy looked away.

Madge nodded to him cheerfully out of the coloured daze around her and said goodnight. He stood a few minutes trying to get the story of the film, his heart parched with terror, then went upstairs.

His mother came into his room, tidied away his clothes, perched his boots by the unused fireplace and then, sitting on the edge of the bed, she watched him.

"Did he make a show of himself," she asked.

"No," he answered.

"Was your Uncle George off with another woman?"

"No, Mama."

"You sure, boy?"

"Yes."

"Yes," she complained softly, shaking out a shirt and folding it over twice, "I don't want the whole world knowing while I remain ignorant."

"No."

Jimmy could see the distorted jealousy, combined with worry, on her face.

"There was no one," he lied, "I promise you."

"Join them," she said to herself, "they're on both sides." Then standing with her back to him in the doorway, holding the knob in one hand and tracing the side wall with the other, she spoke without turning around, "Who is that downstairs?"

"Madge and Stan, that's all."

"Oh, yes, Madge and Stan," she repeated with terrible tenderness, then closed the door quietly behind her.

The warm kitchen floor was alive with beetles when he walked across it barefooted to steal a drink from the fridge. He took a can of goya nectar from the shelf where it sat beside the transparent red snappers, and drank till it flooded his ears. The birdcage was covered by the green curtain and he thought of the cockatiel inside standing up asleep, her head, with its stiff yellow feathers and red bruises, under her tossed wing, like his mother upstairs. He let the car roll, started it in second and drifted down. And because he was alone, he became disorientated, so what should have come to him naturally had to be planned and foreseen.

By seeing the end of the journey before he had begun, all his excitement was lessened, as if he had passed a certain stage in his life that dissipated all that had gone before. The Renault groaned as it climbed the hill to Highgate. He grew terrified of the noise and had to stop, bringing the driving seat forward so that he might have better control of the pedals.

Then the car refused to start.

So, finally, he started in reverse, drove smoothly by her house, turned in the village and stopped high over the city, facing the car back down the hill.

Her house was again in darkness, but there was a veiled light at the bottom of the front door. He did not look up at her window, nearly as if he had forgotten her. Instead he undid the gate and went up the gravel path. The front door was ajar, and from a room further on in the hallway he could hear everyday voices. They were talking about sport and animals. But it was the smell from within the house that made him stop there on the straw mat. He breathed it in, over and over, and looked up the narrow stairs to where her room was, tasting the strangeness and the flickering of shadows along the landing. He thought of her above and what she would think of him were he to enter now and noiselessly ascend from step to step. But he did not move, for whatever happened she must come down of her own free will. He stood there. Then stepped out again and without hesitation pulled the door to behind him. He closed the gate. He looked up at her room. And the more he looked up, the more he became aware of the light in the room, but now he did not know whether it was from outside coming in, or inside coming out. He sat into the car.

And in the silence, like a river about to overflow its banks, he began counting again, so that each number might somehow raise a buttress against the flood that raged about his senses, threatening, with its lusts and jealousies and self-pityings, to sweep him before it across useless places, and he spoke the numbers out loud so that if anyone came they would pass by, knowing he was counting the shapes that fevers leave behind on walls and ceilings, on cars and houses, where shadows no longer reflect the lines of real objects but discard them for the imagined and the unknown, and so he began to unburden himself by mouthing the numbers at the image he held of himself, that it might disappear and, returning with a merry intelligence, admit to the existence of a world other than he had known, where the loved one would always be free of the lover.

So down there on the left, leaving identity aside, is eight

thousand, no hundreds and fifteen, somewhere, there above, eight thousand, no hundreds and sixteen, eight thousand, no hundreds and seventeen, eight thousand, no hundreds and eighteen, eight thousand, no hundreds and nineteen. The man above, eight thousand, no hundreds and twenty. The seagull below, eight thousands, no hundreds and twenty-one. Eight thousand, no hundreds and twenty-two, eight thousand, no hundreds and twenty-three, eight thousand, no hundreds and twenty-four, he rested his head on the steering wheel, hey what are you doing there, man, and now we have another voice, goodnight, eight thousand, no hundreds and twenty-five, and then, what came to his mind next he knew to be wrong and he searched in panic each side of the number in his head for the right one, up and down the scale of all he could remember or see, but once lost, it went adrift and could not be found.

He could not recognize the place where he was.

So, he must start all over.

There was no light in her room. She had not come out the door.

He panicked, began counting, and this time, so that he might not forget where he was, he started on all the animate things he could see, those that could be identified and those that could not, so that his counting might have some reason, but he refused the number of times he thought he saw her appear by the window or the door, for that was foolishness, some numbers were not for counting, and he no longer mouthed the figures in rhyme but at irregular intervals, leaving out sometimes whole centuries; and when he arrived back at random among the tens of thousands, and when he knew everything to be seen in Highgate, from the magnolia spots on plane leaves to the terracotta slates on a stranger's house, the insipid blur of a horse descending behind the elephants, the massive drones of the bull elephants that could have come from a boat on the distant Thames, he allowed the figures to slip away into his consciousness where the counting could continue unabated but without his constant care, and finally, he consigned the crack of light, where her door had stood ajar and he had entered, to his mind, the last sane item and bearing the highest number he had yet reached, then as that last chance receded into forgetfulness, he stopped counting so abruptly that everything lost its shape for a long time to come.

Madge was sitting at the bottom of the stairs when he returned, her head gripped tightly in her hands as if she had suffered some unbearable fright. When she saw him she tried to hide, grow smaller if that was possible, so he sidestepped her, not wanting to breach her loneliness. "Ah, well, see you later, then," she called, and reassured by his presence, with her arms crossed, she hopped up the high steps after him.

The Tenant

IT WAS ONE of those cold Sunday mornings when dismissed Christians came home swiftly from Mass and only packs of good-natured dogs roamed the streets, jumping out on unsuspecting cars.

The heady smell of dinner drifted out through the shutters of the old colonial hotel. The drapes were drawn across an excess of windows that looked down on bleak shopfronts and indifferent private houses. Because of the lack of stimulus from without, the Swanns had filled the foyer and lounge of the hotel with hoards of comfortable retreats and the walls with pictures of streams, rivers and wild life.

The single-roomed bus station was perched down by the real polluted river. The clerk left the *Sunday Independent* cartoons aside when the 12.30 arrived from Dublin, and he and the saloon taxi-drivers gathered around the front of the bus.

Here, in a cold February of the 1960s Mr Franklin stepped down, skirted the offers of the taxi drivers and, changing his two cases from hand to hand every few yards, headed towards the hotel.

In the suburbs, Mr Johnson, lately returned from England, lived with his wife and two sons. He had built the two-storey house himself, plastering the porch with seashells, but gave outside contracts for the plumbing and electricity because he did not want to invite any enmity from those trades. For the first six months after the house was completed he had worked as a petrol pump attendant then moved on to a nice quiet number as a day porter at Swann's Hotel. Everyone believed that Johnson had a fortune put away, but whatever the truth of that rumour, it was conceded that he seemed to have few ambitions left.

On this particular Sunday morning, Johnson was hoovering out the breakfast room before dinner, when he was called to attend a guest who had booked into No. 4.

He first saw Mr Franklin standing soberly in the doorway of the hotel, his hand holding back the lace curtain so that he could see into the street. Each side of him stood two leather cases without stickers or labels, packed with just sufficient wordly goods to suggest no hint of bulk or untidiness. The bottoms of the trousers showing under his coat were pressed and narrow, which was a sign of the times.

"Good morning," said the porter.

"How do you do," remarked Mr Franklin, turning abruptly.

They climbed the heavily carpeted stairs in silence, past the brass gong, and went down the dark corridor where loose boards swayed under their feet like old familiar springs. Mr Johnson swung open the doors of the wardrobe and pulled out all the drawers of the chest. He looked into the waste-paper bin. "Dinner, one to two, tea, half-five to seven, breakfast half-seven to nine," he said, about to pull the door behind him. Mr Franklin seemed to have something more on his mind as he looked around the bedroom.

"Yes?" asked the porter.

"Do you have hot water throughout the day?"

Mr Johnson walked over and turned on the high brass tap in a little sink under the window.

They both watched the water run until the steam arose. The porter nodded, left the room to get on with his cleaning, while the guest knelt by his bed in front of one of his cases and stared impassively at the heavily-patterned wallpaper. Then he took a wad of notes from his inside pocket and counted them with the skill of a cardplayer, his thumb reaching for a watered sponge that wasn't there.

He did not count them again.

He looked out the window at the small miserable town, the fighting jackdaws on the sagging slates with their burden of moss, the flat roof above Woolworth's with pools of water on its dark-green felt. The porter below was emptying rubbish into a colossal bin that stood two hands higher than him. His every movement echoed in the red-bricked alleyway. A rattle of buckets followed the clash of the lid. The twin sounds of the latch lifting and descending.

Mr Franklin opened his cases and began putting away his shirts. He hung his two spotless suits in the old camphor-smelling wardrobe and, perched lightly on the bed in his carpet slippers, began eating a thin ham sandwich, one hand cupped under his chin for the crumbs.

That evening Micko Johnson remarked to his wife, "The new cashier booked in today."

"What is he like?" she asked, turning over a page.

"A strange bird," he mused, "but don't get me wrong, well-mannered."

"Keep in there," she rebuked him.

Next morning, Mr Franklin began work at the Bank of Ireland in Main Street, behind a mahogany counter where the hand-painted floor mosaics stopped and the linoleum began. The work was no more difficult than he had known before. The principles were leaner than those in Dublin, and the complexities few. A coal fire blazed in a yellow-tiled fireplace which was kept going by a small uniformed porter who responded sullenly to orders and kept his own judgements of how things should be run. The manager had an open, liverish face and the movements of an undisciplined army major gone to seed. The world of finance in the small town had made him accept less than the notions he had started with. Interest rates did not change, inflation was unthinkable and the steel vaults were not affected by war or the price of gold, but by the price of livestock and land which rose without indecent haste.

The times were colourless and benign.

The last cashier had been transferred because of a scandal, but, as yet, Mr Franklin was only a temporary replacement, since the transfer had occurred in a hurry lest the tone of the bank should have been affected.

There was no time for Mr Franklin to find his way around. He had to start work immediately.

The first customers avoided him. They searched for help elsewhere, and when they were referred back to the new cashier, they still addressed their transactions over his shoulder to more familiar faces. But he continued to smile and speak in a low democratic voice, so that soon he was accepted as a timid soul, without airs or graces, certain not to grow impatient over complicated figures; and his advice, when he was eventually asked for it, was precise and all-embracing.

The Tenant

That afternoon he approached Swann's for his lunch with an exhilarated step, breathing in the new town like a drug that would always be better than the rest. The townsfolk watched him with anticipation, seeking to find in him the dissipations of his predecessor. At best it was expected of him that he should have irregular habits and the eccentricities of the educated. But his gait was purposeful and only the frequent pinch of his fingers told remotely of an inner life. Nor over lunch did he display any self-consciousness that sees incorrectly the before and after of things; instead he treated each overcooked course with special interest, as if he were being treated to such pleasantries for the first time, and this won the waitress's heart, who told the cook, who told the day porter, of the new cashier's impeccable civility.

"He's a saint," repeated the waitress as she spread a mushed dollop of tinned apple into a bowl of stiff semolina, then in her black frock and white apron, altered at home by herself, she sped to his table, where he waited, handkerchief across his lap and his hands resting positively on the table.

"Thank you," he nodded.

The Bank of Ireland was a stiff, colonial building, contemporaneous with Swann's Hotel itself, belonging to the day when they both overlooked the mud-wall cabins of the town. The barred lower windows were pointed, and the lower frames filled with stained glass. The brass knocker and the letter box were polished excessively by the bank porter because that job enabled him to talk to passers-by. The stone walls were kept an impeccable grey. The manager and his wife lived in the large rooms on the second floor, and here the manager's wife often looked out suspiciously at the precocious life below. In her earlier days she had cut herself off from the social life of the town, but now, intrigued by the persona and bearing of her husband's new recruit, she sent word that he was to be invited up to tea. The other clerks shook their heads wisely.

Mr Franklin told Mr Johnson that the hotel staff need not set a place for him that evening as he was dining out with the manager, Mr Moran.

The porter, having heard the rumours of Mrs Moran's self-enforced isolation, and her probable distress at the activities of the previous cashier, was taken aback.

"That's certainly a boon," said the porter, holding his chin low and a cigarette cupped to his thigh.

Mr Franklin smiled briskly.

The third floor of the bank held old tills from the turn of the century and large unframed photographs of the opening of the bank. Watching the ceremony were animals roped to the carts, with their drivers looking the other way at an approaching band. Files bound with ribbons were stacked from ceiling to floor, and they were flanked by piles of old blue coin bags filled with outdated cheques, large as magazines. There were children's toys and a collection of soldiers who marched in perfect order behind hand-made tanks in a cracked glass case. Two outdated safes, containing some still important material, stood in the old unused servants' rooms, with the maker's name cast in circular fashion around stiff handles that had to be cranked like village pumps before they swung open.

"Here," said Mr Moran, reaching in, "is the memoranda of our first deposit."

Mr Franklin held the frayed piece of parchment up to the light. "They have amalgamation plans afoot for us above, I believe," whispered the manager. "I hear talk of it," replied Mr Franklin delicately. He admired with a nod of his thin skull the faded handwriting, each small figure sketched with the reverence given to millions, and the symbols for sterling like musical notations giving what came after the appearance of poetry, and above all the name of the parent bank, their present employer who might any day merge with the enemy, drawn with heiroglyphic intensity, and then each side, the brown scales of justice.

"An important document," agreed Mr Franklin. "They took things serious then."

"They had their priorities right," the manager said, "and treated everyone with the same courtesy."

"Of course," Mr Franklin summed up, "we were dealing with less customers then."

"That's why," affirmed the manager, "my predecessors could

afford to throw nothing away."

They descended the dimly lit stairs, one behind the other, their grey heads bent slightly forward as they searched for the next hidden step.

The ceiling of the living-room, burdened down with brightly painted plaster fruits, loomed like a frantic reflection of life elsewhere. "Yes," Mrs Moran explained, "It was the governor's town house." The floor was carpeted in thick autumn gold. At the northern end, armchairs and settee sat by the fireplace, by the door cane tables and chairs.

The manager's wife had already prepared a chicken salad which Mr Franklin found unsettling for that time of the year.

"It is a wretched town in which to buy decent lettuce," Mrs Moran said over tea.

It did not escape her notice that Mr Franklin was avoiding his lettuce. "The lettuce here," she continued, trying to bluff him with her small ink-spotted eyes, "is forever dried up and inhabited by slugs too countless to mention." Mr Franklin lifted up his knife and fork and, with a lashing of salad cream, again attached the limp leaves. "The lettuce leaf direct from the garden is God's bounty," she ended the discourse which had been directed unflinchingly at the cashier's bowed head, which rose intermittently, only to refuse further allocations. "The Government leaves us no choice," remarked the Manager, "but to concede to the foreign Industrialist what should be going to our own people. The blackguards abscond with the grants and leave unworkable second-hand machinery behind them." His wife, with a small cough, gave thanks. Mr Franklin made no sign that he thought little of the small store she set by her cooking, or that he understood the nervousness that kept her aloof from her fellow man, for he could read all these mal-functions in the eyes of her silent husband, who afterwards layered his bread with strawberry jam in lieu of dessert, an act Mr Franklin found impossible to follow, despite goodwill, acquiescence or his decayed sweet tooth.

"I can envisage that chap,' said Mr Moran when Franklin was gone, "becoming a permanent fixture below."

"I could make nothing of him," his wife untruthfully replied. Mr Franklin, wrapped in his overcoat, sat reading in his hotel room from the collected works of John Ruskin. Before going to bed he went downstairs to warm his thin shins before the lounge fire. A group of men finishing their drinks were sitting in a circle around the glowing grate while their secretary summed up their party's affairs. But Johnson the porter was behind the small bar. "Did it go well?" asked Johnson in a sly intimate fashion, as if he and the cashier from that first morning had entered into some undignified partnership. "It was an interesting evening," replied Mr Franklin. "I bet you could put them boys straight," said the porter, indicating the group by the fire while he spun a glass in his hands. Mr Franklin savoured the responsibility his job gave him by offering the porter a modest smile. "The man before you did not leave things any easier," said Johnson, raising his eyebrows in a further show of uncalled for sympathy. Mr Franklin said nothing. "Hold the fort, then," said the porter, "because I know what you are after."

Nervously, Mr Franklin stood by the bar while the porter slipped away into the kitchen. Mr Franklin, ashamed of his carpet slippers and white exposed ankles, felt an eternity go by. The porter returned with a piping hot enamel hotwater bottle.

"I know," said Mr Johnson, in his slight English accent, "How to look after my guests."

So began a nightly ritual that continued throughout the rest of the spring months. Whatever step Mr Franklin took he was sure to run into the porter who seemed to work inordinate hours at the hotel. While Mr Franklin himself, trying to hide a deep well of impatience that troubled his very being, worked late hours by his desk, bringing troublesome accounts up to date and sorting out new business without resort to the old class distinctions. For it would be unthinkable for the manager or the old clerks to see their bank as merely a shop that sold money. They still treated workers with the customary disdain, leading them into the inner sanctuary that had about it the stiff, unwelcoming air of a confessional. They had power over the people because they knew their secrets, and the sinners would emerge from these meetings, rebuffed and withdrawn. It was a practice Mr Franklin disapproved of, for the lower-class Catholic trade with the bank was on the increase because of the new flurry of public relations, and this new business needed careful handling. And the new public image also meant the increased employment of women and the big question was, would they wear their own clothes or a uniform? It was hard to believe that money would now be channelled through non-masculine hands. And after the women, to the utter bewilderment of the older clerks, would come the computers.

And after that would follow all the chaos of the common world.

The male parental care of previous banking generations was at risk, the whole family of banking men being exposed to lesser lights, in a time when asylums were sacred and promiscuity shared outside the home, and it was the talk of strikes that drove Mr Moran further into his shell, so that Mr Franklin was now not only permanent but indispensable, and it would be on his bachelor's shoulders and prematurely grey head the burden of approaching modernity would sit, meaning that he must like women and like machines that were programmed to undermine his domain by calculation and grievances beyond telling.

"You are one of ours," the little wizened bank porter told Mr Franklin one day. He tipped his skull with a knowing finger. "I can tell."

The cashier's evenings were spent either reading or working. There was plenty of time for frivolity in the years ahead, and like the manager and his wife, he rarely graced the streets of the town with his presence. He was fitted out for a new suit in McKenna's which was much to his liking, with the most perfect waistcoat he ever had, and lapels thin as knives. In old sheds down the market yard at night he could hear from his room the youth of the town dancing to the Beatles, and market days mountainy farmers slouched on the chairs of Swann's eyeing him for weaknesses, then in the late evening the lonely Indian doctors sat around the piano, drinking cold gins and tonic, while a local drunk pounded the keys, and bought round after round for them because they were different. Flour lorries vied with Esso tankers on the narrow streets, so that all traffic came to a stop, till the lorries mounted the footpaths driving the pedestrians before them.

"I'll tell you what," exclaimed Mr Johnson with exaggerated

courtesy one bright summer's evening as he chased along the hotel corridor with a broom, "why don't you move in with us?"

Mr Franklin spun the key in the loose lock of his bedroom door.

"Sleep on it," continued the porter. "My wife can cook good as the best of them and you'll find us half the price of the hotel."

"I'm quite happy here," answered Mr Franklin at a loss.

"Just bear it in mind, all right?" the porter said unwavering. "You of all people should know the right and wrong of these things."

Later that week, Mr Franklin took a walk out in the country, identifying modes of pleasure that might sustain him as his nature homed in on the need for domestic security, and Mr Johnson's house was pointed out to him by a roadsweeper. "You can't miss it," said the roadsweeper, dipping his hand in a stiff wave, "It's neither one thing or another." The house, bare of trees and shrubbery, seemed to have newly emerged from the sea with a coating of barnacles. The cockles were of the type that coat heavy lamps. The garden was pitted with cement and building materials, and the cut into the hill was still not healed, except for pockets of light grass and clumps of builders' poppies.

Muddy water ran across the road from shores not properly realigned and little sandalled footprints that ran down the path must have been left by the porter's youngest son before the cement had set.

The house looked somehow innocent, in a word, bravely decent.

On the day he moved there Mrs Johnson explained to Mr Franklin that only families that returned from England had the gumption to take the stranger in.

"The rest," she explained, "think it's beneath them."

She was a small balding woman, who trotted rather than walked, and spoke, like her husband, ahead of herself, as if all introductory conversation was unseemly. Her quiet withdrawn son looked as if he, too, had been on this earth before and stored up unaccountable vengeances from his previous stay, though now, with his steps forever firmly planted on the path, it seemed he was treating this present existence with more seriousness.

The eldest lad, Mrs Johnson acknowledged, was bright but full of stops and starts. They were climbing the stairs. They were touring the rooms. "His father got him into McArdle's," she beat Mr Franklin's pillow, "because there was no way of continuing his schooling here without the Irish language, and there he'll stay till he can better himself."

The first thing Mr Franklin noticed in his newly painted room was that he could dispense with his overcoat and that he would not be awoken by jackdaws. The radiators, set into roughly plastered holes, sent out a constant traffic of nauseating heat. Against the blinded window a second-hand desk with roller and pens had been placed, where, the porter explained, Mr Franklin could go over his figures. A statue of the Virgin Mary stood in a recess with a hideous viper baring its fangs under her white rounded feet, that stood on what? Perhaps a half-globe of an uncoloured, unfinished world. And the great joy was the walk, benign in good weather, exhilarating when the wind got up, from the house into the town when Mr Franklin would receive a variety of greetings from all and sundry, who among themselves, were astonished by such exact timekeeping.

The bank by now had begun to tackle the forthcoming formidable task of decimalization.

Thinking in tens rather than twelves was driving the elder clerks to desperation and they feared the chaos ahead of them in a couple of years, as another man might fear to be thrown out of his home. The new order would restrict advancement, amalgamation limit superiority. But having no other stability in the world except his work, Mr Franklin relished the architectural cleanness of the metrical system, the satisfaction of teasing out patterns that brought new areas of the mind into play. He kept the decimalization tables always by him and his only sentiment was that he saw very early on that, like the half-crown, the old silver sixpence would have to go.

Soon Mr Franklin's reserve, and sometimes curt replies were his solitiude in his room to be interrupted, became unsettling for Mrs Johnson. She heard stories of bank clerks who were bedwetters and some who were thieves, so each day after his departure she checked the cashier's bed and desk, but everything was above board, except for a certain briefcase that was always kept locked, which seemed more disloyal than dishonest. Mr Franklin noticed, but took no umbrage at her searching, for he had long ago accepted the necessity of others rechecking your credentials and your figures, and in case she might be fretting over the briefcase, from then on he left it open on the bed. This demoralized Mrs Johnson. And sometimes, when he sat with her in the downstairs room to smile blandly at the Dave Allen show, she could hardly contain herself.

It became necessary for her to wait till her tenant had retired to his room before she could talk at ease to her husband.

"He's neat, he's tidy," she said one evening, "but there is something evil about that man."

"What are you saying?" asked Johnson.

"I don't," she muttered, "like to be left alone in the house with him."

"Well then," said Johnson, "you'll not be too happy to know that I transferred our account to him today."

"That's the last straw," she said, unable to bear the thought of an individual knowing the secrets of her purse, without once acknowledging his debt.

Mr Johnson gave up his night shift at the bar, financially leaving them where they were before they had taken Franklin in. His wife's meals, which had improved immensely on the arrival of the cashier, were now served up in a desultory fashion, the soup was thin and buttons of undissolved Bisto floated in the now frequent stews. The porter began repeating after meals and endured excruciating bouts of indigestion, and his only consolation was that the cashier must have been going through the same suffering as himself. Franklin, for his part, had further complicated things by taking a liking to the eldest son, Ronnie, who would sometimes accompany the cashier into his place of work, and then pass his father somewhat arrogantly as he swept the footpath outside Swann's. In the house Ronnie waited on the cashier hand and foot and sought his advice where before he would have gone to his father. Thus the parents had to curtail and expurgate criticism of their unwitting tenant in front of the son for fear he might carry it back.

So, at last, their only privacy in the new house was in the bed with its electric blanket, where their first intimacies had begun.

"Your Mister Benjamin," said Mrs Johnson ironically after one especially exasperating evening, "will have to go."

But in his room Mr Franklin was enjoying all these evenings, while his eviction was plotted across the landing, an unwarranted feeling of satisfaction and peace. Ronnie would pick books off his shelf and bring them back filled with cigarette coupons as markers. Aerial photography was Mr Franklin's joy, because he held that what is seen from above mitigates all that's seen from below and gives us a grasp of what the future might hold, when the common traveller would have recourse to wheels only for landing. And how our forefathers, because of their sympathies for the skies, built forts that looked upwards, as well as across, dangerous and uncharted territories.

A night in September came when the bank's annual do was being held in the White Horse. Mr Franklin went, accompanied by the Morans. So the Johnson family had the house to themselves except for Ronnie who was off dancing at the Wonderland Ballroom. While the clerks and their women tore at the usual turkey, the Johnson's had beautiful lamb chops in parsley and honey sauce. Their house and family seemed immune from any unreasonable intrusion, their joy and security untrammelled and all thought of the cashier was dismissed from their minds, his thin frame and soapy smell forgotten.

Mr Johnson repeated some humorous stories from his day at the hotel. He copied once again the cook's walk across the kitchen, and the waitress's habit of leaning forward and picking stray fluff off her companion's coat as she gossiped. Mrs Johnson, during the pauses, recalled earlier unhappier days in London when they were getting together the pennies that had built their present vulnerable fortress, giving her husband that steely glare that made him feel responsible for all the woes that had befallen them.

Then, after midnight, they heard light steps on the stairs.

"That's the bugger, Mick," laughed Mrs Johnson, "inhospitable as ever."

"I think you are too hard on him," said the porter.

Somehow, having the clerk back above increased their joviality. They sat on well past the hour when they would normally have gone to bed, making extra cups of tea which Mick laced with brandy. It was time for them to discover old photographs, but to avoid sentimentality which got you nowhere fast, so Mick reckoned. Whining was out for the traveller. You just took the scaffolding down floor by floor, so that when you had spun off the last nut and dropped the final bar you would never dream that that very morning, you had stood up there abreast of the chimney tops. Or it could be, Mrs Johnson was saying, having lost the child you'd carried three months down the toilet, you just changed your knickers and set off for work, for what was the sense of crying, I ask you? They moved from chair to chair telling their stories. Once, coming in from the kitchen with more nourishment, Mrs Johnson heard a rumpus above. The noise ended. She brought her husband out into the hall. They listened a while and again the noise started with an awkward rhythm that unnerved them both with its familiarity. She pulled her husband up the stairs, who at that moment sought refuge from what would only demean them both. "God," she said giggling, "I'd love to see the auld hure at it." They listened outside Franklin's door and the soft coo of a woman's voice was unmistakable.

"Now," she whispered into her husband's ear, "You have him."

"Oh Christ," he answered, drawing back.

"Under our roof," she forced his elbow forward.

Mick pulled himself together, and as his wife swung open the door, he reached for the light and the two of them fell drunkenly into the room. And there, speechlessly, they beheld their eldest son, draped in Mr Franklin's pink sheet, whispering softly into a girl's ear something that would be always a secret to them both, while, astride her, his buttocks gently rocked.

"Get out!" roared Ronnie. "Get out!"

The incident in his room was never reported to Mr Franklin, but, unwittingly, he took the blame, for Mrs Johnson treated him now to an irrevocable silence. He seemed to eat more often at Moran's, sometimes the Wednesday and Friday of every week, where the manager and himself sought to know through various arguments, bolstered up with sherry, whether the current fear in Ireland of the International Monetary Fund was justified, or proper to a legendary nationalism that fears progress. They discussed whether genuine political administrators had been superceded by personalities who might not understand the proper tenets of political behaviour and therefore spend valuable time seeking revenge against their opposites, rather than considering the Western economic world which had supported them through their every crisis, and only exacted from them basic loyalty.

"The party system as practised here," said Mr Moran, "leaves a lot to be desired. We bankers who control them in the long run cost less to employ. But," and he waved that incorrigible finger, "the family must hold together."

"The loyalists are getting bad press," said Mr Franklin regarding the recent minor disturbances in the North.

"They will have forgotten about it by the time Christmas is over," the manager tapped the fire with a brass poker, "mark my words, but either way it's not us will have to pay."

"That itself," said Mr Franklin.

The cashier was enjoying the thrust of the customers and come Christmas it was he gave out the small plastic calendars, saying with a smile, "They are good for peeling frost off your windscreens." The bank made a contribution to the Christmas tree which was erected in the market square, and they contributed towards the lights, which were strung across the main street like bunting, falling a little every night toward the street below. Mr Franklin bought a set of crystal glasses for the Morans, sherry and whiskey for the Johnsons, to Ronnie *The Guinness Book of Records* and a cowboy suit for the young lad. But now he could detect the barely disguised hostility in the house.

"You don't mind," Mr Johnson had at last brought himself to speak, "we would like to spend Christmas alone."

"Of course," answered Mr Franklin, "I'll take my things and move into Swann's."

"But have you no place to go, say, in Dublin for the holiday?" asked the porter, dreading any adverse criticism that might accrue from the cashier leaving their home.

Mr Franklin said nothing.

On the twenty-third he went with his two cases to the hotel where late that evening, Mr Moran, for the first time abroad in a local hostelry where he had no duty to perform, joined him at the bar. Mr Franklin, freed of the constrictions of the house and glad to be back in the privacy of the old rooms, was in a celebratory mood, and glad to have somehow found his own level. And while the two men were there, in a quiet recess inside the door under an old fatigued lampshade, surrounded by green upholstery and quiet pictures of deers and sheep, Ronnie arrived very flustered and breathless. Before Mr Moran could extract himself from what was a mortifying situation for him, and private for them, the boy blurted out, "They should not have done that."

"But Ronnie," said Mr Franklin, "I'm only staying here for the Christmas."

"I know what they are at," said Ronnie, "I know them."

"Sit down," said the manager, "and let me get you something."

Mr Franklin looked wildly after the manager, knowing that the transgressions of his predecessor were still fresh in both their minds.

Knowing no better and having received no instructions, Mr Moran returned from the bar with a glass of whiskey. Ronnie thanked him and said, "They are trying to humiliate Mr Franklin." "Indeed," said Mr Moran. "That's enough now, Ronnie," said the cashier. The lad sat there in the embarrassing silence, then lifting the whiskey he threw it all back in one mouthful. His eyes watered as he gagged. He clapped his hands, made for the bar and returned before Mr Franklin had time to explain.

"There is another round on its way," said Ronnie.

"You've got to go home now," said the cashier.

"You are doing Mr Franklin no good, you know," said the manager.

The cashier's face grew ashen, and in a high-pitched whisper he said to Ronnie, who was looking from one to the other, "Go home, home, home!" adding with a rap on the table that carried across the lounge: "Now!" A few moments passed, "Please."

96

Banished Cock ~~Misfortune~~

THE HOUSE that Saul lived in.

While the children slept there, outside it rained. The whole night long. Though it was warm and brown among the damp shiny chestnuts, the weather had opened under the shadows of the rambling trees. Everything was falling. The thump of chestnuts on the soft floor of the night. And the insects thrived down there in the caves of leaves. Eileen slept facing east, young child limbs learning to fly and the people of Belfast looking up in wonder. The duchess hopped along the stairs, past the dusty quiet of McFarland's door where the mother turned often in her sleep down an empty and alien past, and the cat sat up beside the small steamy window with the lead stripes to catch her breath, where the magpies had chewed the new putty. Listening to the water swirling over the stones and the loose gate banging in the lower meadow. And when little Tom coaxed her down onto the bed, she put her washing away and jumped like a little deer.

"Here, puss," he said and she stretched out one long paw.

For whatever reason the house might fall, the sleeping McFarland would build again with a sense of adventure anywhere north of the lakes and in good time, son of Saul, master builder of Fermanagh country but by pneumonia put away while tended by his wife Olive, Glan woman and descendant of J. O'Reilly who danced once with flax in his trousers, and though nominally Christian died in foreign and pagan lands fighting an unjust war, but McFarland sensing the lie of the land grew away from a sense of guilt or desire for power and prayed that the haphazard world would not destroy his family so well grounded among the moralities of chance and nature, if one could remain loyal to the nature of a people and not the people themselves, for whatever reason the house might fall.

The door opened onto the fields.

All round, that silence and damp air of expectancy after the eerie rasp of the storm had blown over.

Judy, his wife, cooked over a single gas jet in the leafy half-light, for the electricity black-out was at its worst and it seemed to McFarland like one of those early mornings years ago when he had risen in the cold to feed the cattle and heard the groan of the house and Saul's asthmatic breathing overhead. Still the echo of the sessions that had gone on through the night when he was a child. The children put on two sets of jumpers and climbed into their boots under the stairs, and Eileen picked up a toy soldier knocked over by the foot of the father as he went round the back to examine the roof for missing slates. Soft Chinese music of the rain on glass and leaves, lightly touched cymbals, ducks crashing onto the waters, the primitive crane stretching her awkward wings in a lone high flight, the land below so cold and misty it looked as if a healing frost had settled.

Little Tom chased Eileen sideways through the mist to the end of the garden, among the penitent crumbling apple trees, in her new frock and washed hair and everywhere a silent promise that she might be well.

"The night it being dark in my favour," the father sang fretfully to himself in the boot of the car, unconcerned about the helicopter that flew over the house and scattered the birds that a moment before had been strolling along the hedges. Humming a reel like a dream he was trying to remember, McFarland, out of an incapacity to deal with the extravagance of small details, involved his wife and children in discovering the pattern from last year for fitting in the case, instruments and bags. He scraped the fiddle bow thoughtfully under his chin and sang it backwards and forward across his ear as he went through the mathematics. Talking in a holiday voice to nuts and screws and old newspapers, while his wife reasoned with the children, losing her patience. Will Byrne, the sentinel of the hill, his brother murdered at his door, watched their activities with benign speculation as he lay against an old railing from which he propelled himself every few seconds and took a quick low whistle, escaping from the past for a few excruciating moments.

"You get in the back with your mother," the father said and little Tom put the cat down reluctantly in the shed and dropped a chicken bone temptingly into her dish. She was sitting at a ladylike distance away, upset by the jamming of the doors and all those signs of departure. He hid another bigger bone behind the shed after whistling down the fields, watching a weasel drink water from the cup of a leaf among the chopped timber. The duchess suddenly attended to her wardrobe. The soft scuffle of leaves and harness. After they had all driven away, the dog, with pebbles hanging from his coat, came in mumbling because he had been forgotten and the cat flew up onto the rafters, while above her the rain slanted to the west.

"What'll we sing?" asked little Tom.

The father looked up to heaven, his musical children vain and happy by turns, his child wife looking steadfastly silently ahead as she always did when they journeyed together, always heading off into some fitful future, living off the excitement of leaving something intangible behind and the wheels on the road had a life of their own. Edging down the lane, the dark purple of the sloes, sour grapes, the blackberries tidily hung between the bronze leaves and yellow roots of the hedge. Lakes, a darker purple than the sloes away below the chestnut trees. A soldier's jeep was parked on the crossroads, guns cocked. "You can learn to live with anyone," Saul had said, "it's imperial to me!" And McFarland, reared amongst a series of foreign and local escapades, took everywhere his copies of the Arctic and Antarctic voyages. "Irish musicians are a crowd of drunken children," Judy said to him once as they drank Guinness from a bedroom sill in a boarding-house. "I suppose it wasn't what the Lord wanted," he said eventually, away from her down to the Roscommon men strolling through the riotous, melancholy music. Still, tucked under his elbow as he sauntered through the dark deserted streets of Belfast where the men drank gin and the women drank whiskey, he always had his copy of Scott's final trip up the frozen Pole, a book he had read many many times and still felt the same harsh ecstacy the explorers must have experienced when, worn to the bone of humanity, they discovered that the Norweigians had been there before them. And the other explorers held down by the winter, frozen and breathless and singing songs under the snow.

The family drove through the clouds and Friday, the dog, chased round the farm for the scents that were fast fading.

Eileen lit the matches for her father's cigarettes, cupping her awkward hands like the men do in the yard to save the light from the wind. Like she was reading the future from the palms of her hands, stained with the juices of the early-morning leaves where so many faces were hidden. And all round strange wet farmhouses, the finely cropped trees of the north, cut like mushrooms or birds settling with wings tucked, fine cars in the driveways along the wide fields, the distinctive roadway signs, the extinct lorries. Behind the sheds like railway carriages and over the hills the grim Norse-like churches. Going over the bridges there was a great empty feeling beneath your heart as the car rose. Like a roof lifting off a house. Her mother's agitated face when their uncle threatened. If time could wait. Once Eileen's stomach turned sick, mesmerized by the sudden looseness of her limbs, her head swaying. McFarland walked her up and down a laneway off the main road with his tolerant musical strides, while overhead the trees joined branches in the mist that was blinding the islanders as they rowed ashore on the flooded Erne, adjusting to the repeated deaths beside the blue frosted lakes, at night the cool drinks, hands dextrous at cards. She hated these moments that she had no control over. But it was better to be sick and let her eyes film over with tears for a moment than arrive bleary-eyed and fatigued after dosing herself with the heavy languorous pills she took as a child that made her memory falter. Her hair was cut so short for her face that she showed pain too easily. And she was irked by Tom's cheerfulness behind her in the car, her instincts left in him.

"A big girl like you won't find the time passing," his voice above her, afraid of any weakness that might handicap their security, humming and smoking in the mist with his hand on her shoulder, we'll be there in no time. "We'll be there in no time," he said.

And that's how little Tom, anxious to laugh, attracting laughter, succeeded in getting into the front seat beside his father to pull the window down and trail his hands near the low trees that flew by like the wind, too quick even for his eyes to catch, and wave at the Customs man as they crossed the last ramp and headed down the bad easy roads, the Leitrim-Cavan border where traditions had survived even the Famine itself, a roofless countryside without trees or soldiers or gunfire at night but the road through the frost-shattered mountains and stray rain-filled clouds, the bilberry bushes and cotton grass. And Sandy Byrne and Friday were leaping through hedges and streams on their way to the village after Old Byrne had cursed the skyline and chased them from his house with a broom. McFarland's eyes were fading, he grieved sometimes for them in the early morning when his vision was hazy like that shortness of breath, and now he was aware of Tom watching him squeeze his eyes, concentrate, slow down and take the centre of the road. After the humours of Ballyconnell they crossed the dry streams where the railway lines had been lifted and sold to the Congo by order of an ecumenical government, here several of his mother's people had flagged down a train and never been seen again, going away with a wisp of smoke and single words in the old Irish. Among the Chinese and gunpowder, among poets and moneygrabbers his grandfather had been there for the driving of the last spike on the Great Pacific Railway till he fell down a frozen thirty-foot falls, his dogs screaming in terror below him and all over the snowswept Canadian valley.

"Tisin' no wonder this is the wee county that Sean Maguire sprang from," the father said, remembering, and thought of the boy in the gap and the lady's top dress and the day he had climbed here with Saul and had a nose-bleed on the mountain.

They left behind the pagan air of Glan, grey damp farms surrounded by cluttered rusy galvanized sheds, washing blowing in the garden, a pump on the road that nobody used, cottages with the thatch sunk in the middle. A huge aerial. The mother slept lazily, hearing Bach's Fantasy and Fugue on her husband's tape and she longed to lean out and draw someone close to her for a while, for someone, she said, tapped her on the shoulder naming various schoolchildren she had taught in Belfast, tall mousy-haired children who hardly ever talked or did in a rush and called to her house whispering angrily, and as her head bobbed against the rear seat she never saw her husband smile boyishly at her in the mirror. And Eileen copied her mother going to sleep, glancing through half-closed eyes at the blue-aproned women, sweeping, washing down their steps and the men crossing the streets with a multitude of different steps, their breath flying behind them. After the trip to Athlone the fiddle quietened, the bodhran settled, trees were down everywhere after the big wind. At various times they came across groups of men standing round with saws under their arms and greatcoats hung up on the side of a ditch. The mist was lifting like the curtain in the Town Hall. They saw the first house in Connaught. They heard the musical priest. And while the sky cleared the family ate next a stone wall, sharing the air with an odd horse that had been looking at the same spot in a gorse haggard for days. Thousands of sewage pipes were piled on the footpaths, a gate opened into a new lake. "The bit of food," Saul had said, "it's like the man begging, it will take you to the next door." And the Shannon had turned the streams into wild dancing streams, sheughs filled with wild water that stranded the cows who wandered about ankle-deep in the muck searching for grass. At last, when they entered the city, a Fresian calf with a white star on his forehead and white back legs stopped the car in the middle of the road and peered in with large blinking enquiring eyes. "A white-headed calf is very hard on the beast," he'd said, "turn him if you can, I'm the queer quack myself."

Peace is not necessary here, she heard that and . . . these people would rather endure. Who was it? Was it him? And again. I think it was St Patrick started this campaign. Was it drunk together on the boat to Belfast, collecting stolen timber from his brother on the docks, his fat belligerent brother who could kill, or was it on another day not in a boat but crossing the road in hot weather when traffic was heavy? My young saintly maidenly unmarried sister sleeping with a Quaker in that deserted bullet-peppered block of flats, oh my sister how sometimes I miss your crusade for there's nothing left for me but to become a victim who at the end of all resources admits nothing.

"Where are we now?" the mother said, wakening.

"Timbuktu," the boy said.

"You so and so," the mother said, ruffling his hair.

"I just combed that out a wee minute ago," said Eileen and she flicked out her own short hair, the holiday at last for real, trying to create some dancing curls, and patted down her fresh autumn dress and knocked the mud of the fields from her shoes, spread out her toes to release the sweet stiffness of the journey from her body, the stifling impression of having gone nowhere till she smelt the roots of the sea, the girl in her gliding down as Ennis slowed the pipes.

Her father closing his eyes gratefully as he stopped the car.

Slates littered the streets of Galway.

Shopkeepers picked their way through the debris, gesticulating and looking up at the sky like sleepwalkers. The scene was obscenely familiar to the family from the north who felt for a moment slightly superior in their ability to deal with chaos, death, laughter at death. The family booked into a boarding house that looked out on a river that ran floundering under heavy stone bridges into the salmon sea, and the nervous landlady was filled with small talk about the storm, as a man held a ladder against the side of the building and his apprentice fought off cramp as he took a perilous path across the roof. The family listened with hidden humour to the stray southern accents, as men shouted encouragement to the climber from the street below. Little Tom mimicking. The boarding house began with a big room, advancing in smaller rooms till it ended in a tiny toilet perched over the river. They spoke self-consciously of the weather and Judy glared at the son of the house who watched Eileen with cold mischievous lust as the girl stood downstairs at the discordant piano fingering the keys in time to the waves of the sea, that same rhythm in her hands as was in her eyes when they had sat in the deserted concert halls in Belfast and she was husbandless, to listen to the orchestra practising the songs of Fauré and the tiny early piano pieces of Mozart such a long time ago.

And Friday had found the bone at the back of the shed and took it down to the edge of the stream, where he drank out of his questioning reflection in the damp mossy shadows where the hesitant rain and leaves still fell.

The slow earth.

"I'll be back early," said McFarland when everything was settled and kisses had been handed round.

"God, oh God man, foolish promises," she answered him and he smilingly pursed his lips and shook his shoulders and with his fiddle case went down to a pub where the barman was a retired monk and sung songs of Napoleon and Aquinas, tapping and patting his companions down.

When first in Portaferry they crossed hands Eileen was a small delighted baby, who had to travel each day by car with her mother to school and the child never cried but lay listless for hours in the nursery, with its high windows that were not for looking through. And when he and Judy married, the child tottered quietly into the small church in autumn and laughed away brown-eyed at her mother looking so serious. For those first few weeks Judy tired easily of the endless sessions and retired early, leaving him alone among a bunch of new emptied musicianors. And as the constant assault of songs and music wore away with his first advances, and they learned each other's ways and the way of the child, she was no longer like a false note in a slow air returning and returning. She showed none of his cunning reticence, was eager to slip into a thousand excitable abstractions. Yet how many towns had they got so drunk in the world might end, playing squash in the early morning handball alleys to soothe a hangover, her fine excited accent a mixture of cynicism and distance. Because the city restrained people, or so he believed, it would have been customary for her sophistication to endure some rural cynicism but in this instance it was his nature gave way, slipping away into a thousand nearly familiar impressions. The complexity attracted him, the adventure of a perfume alien to his sheets, the lane to the door.

Cupping his man-root in her hand, old and awkward gamblings, and she saying slow and he for all his mock heroics learning for the first time the body's music, lightly touched cymbals that rocked them both away.

Red berries next the house, and the sycamore releasing a thousand revolving wings.

Judy brought the children for a long walk on the pier till evening caught them in an early long blue light like the sheen from a silk curtain and they strolled and ran back restlessly to the house. Not that Salthill was beautiful but ugly and plain and yet it was a necessary outing for them all although she was uncertain that any of them might feel release, know the difference in such a short time for they had burrowed down so deep in anxiety that happiness was nearly hysterical. Little Tom's cheeks were warm and Eileen's hair had blown and blown in the wind and they were tired as kings now one day had ended. Judy had grown used to being on her own. In Belfast they had worked apart, she driving out of the city each

morning to Lisburn to teach and he heading off in a blue van to
some new disaster area. And after the sudden move to the old
house and the death of the old man they were suddenly thrown into
each other's company most of the day, like young lovers, finding
themselves grown strange to each other as if their previous work
had sustained some missing link. But one could not but feel
relieved yet cowardly after being released from the rows of terraced
houses. Back in their room with the wasting wallpaper and plastic
flowers, the landlady's family downstairs watching the Saturday
film on television, Tom turned bad-tempered and started to argue,
pulling Eileen away from the ukelele she was playing. The invisible
stars that blind each other. The boy started to hammer the bed
with his fists and the girl squeezed her hands against her face
screaming, while below the television was lowered.

"Stop. Stop," she screamed.

"Ya wanna see a wee bitch," he shouted.

"Leave me alone."

"Stop. Both of ye," yelled Judy.

I can hardly survive any more, thought Judy. Oh nature, nature
who left out my instinct for self-survival and gave me this grudging
betrayal of selfishness instead. When she finally quietened them
down, they sulked but with the confidence of children who know
for what they are crying. "Tomorrow is Sunday," she said, "and in
the morning we'll all travel out to Spiddal and you'll play your
whistle, Tom, for Furaisti and Pete with the bent nose will be
there." Tom was the easiest to bring back, to forgive in a slow
mechanical way the world that threatened to overwhelm him. "It
will be more wonderful than any Fleadh. Yes. And you have no
more school for a fortnight, maybe more." "Will the flute player be
there from England," Tom proffered slowly, "the one who wears
the bicycle clips?" "Yes. Aye. All your father's friends."

"Sleep now ye pair."

And Friday was sitting quietly in the shed beside the duchess
who occasionally looked up at him and the night was there too
except there was no sound, only the sharp cries of the nightbirds
from down the fields.

"That's a lovely daughter you've got there," the landlady said
when Judy opened the door to see who was tiptoeing annoyingly

across the landing. Then to silk she washed herself, her first warm bath for months under the watchful eye of the awful blue staring fish and afterwards she draped herself luxuriously before a small electric fire. The glow from her flesh pleased her as did the silence and the small breaths of the sleeping. When she had left Belfast she had sworn she would never live in a city again, not for a day, but Galway she never really accepted as a city, it was more like a big drifting market town. She and her husband were changing, she knew. In Belfast they were satisfied politically, in that their bodies, like anyone else's, could stop a bullet, but living so close to the south was a totally new beginning, a loveplay, something they had forgotten as she had forgotten that in the south what appeared trivial, negative to her was a natural way of life for a people unaffected by war. But her spirit had once enlarged, as her sister's now had. Still she worried about their farmhouse in Fermanagh constantly, even when she went to the village with the kids she always searched the now familiar trees for smoke, as if in a way she needed a ritual, a gradual dismemberment.

Eileen turned in her sleep.

The wind in the wires outside reminded Judy of home, like the sound of distant geese; she rubbed her body in front of the fire as the evening drew on.

"Politics is the last thing in the world I want to hear about," said McFarland in a pub where he was the centre of attraction as he laid his fiddle down. "The very last thing."

"Give us a slow air," someone interrupted in Salthill as they went from "Toss the Feathers" to "The Flowers of Spring". And the bank manager danced to the tune.

"Everybody in the north wants to get on TV or into politics," a fisherman just in off the trawlers joked in The Largeys where an Irish soldier was playing the pipes in the backroom.

"Galway never changes."

"*Ni bhíonn ac súil amháin ag na nGael anois*,"* said Furaisti softly as they sat ruminating under Conaire in the square and watched a peculiar crowd spreading out from the railway station

*The Irish see through only one eye now.

after arriving on the last train from Dublin. McFarland was restless, spending money recklessly. Saul had said, "If I died tonight wouldn't you heel up the clothes and the money, and say didn't he hold on to it tight." And he had left nothing but the view from the hill. McFarland remembered his own youth as warmth under a slated roof from the heavy rain, a vague wish on the side of a lake, and now returning years later to the house built like a church with its arched porch and stained-glass windows taken by bicycle from Donegal, he was learning the names for sounds he was born into, a tern fleeing from the rushes, milk churns rattling over the evening echo of the lake, a pheasant remembering the balls in her tail running over the mossy earth and perching on a fence to allow her scent bubble over the dogs, a perch bent in the scale-wet hands of his son. Oh history is a great time-saver, a repellent against honest thought. There was no release, not like the falling release of a larch breaking at last under the swing of a steady axe, the shivers showering the earth.

"You know, Furaisti, you could hardly make ceiling laths from the trees in these parts," he said.

"Have you put down any vegetables the year?" asked Furaisti.

"No. Next year for certain," he answered.

The dog slept by the cat in the shed and once he awoke and chased some shots off into the dark and the duchess stirred and smiled when he returned and sank beside her in the straw.

The radiators had filled the room with heavy cumbersome heat when Eileen heard the bomb open the sky in her sleep. A god filling in his time that she darted from on the verge of frightened dreams. She sank beneath the bedclothes when she awoke, silent awhile till, as her panic grew more terrible, she called to her mother in the expressionless dark. Judy came in naked from the other room and wiped the blood from her bewildered daughter's face. In this strange house, even for a day, we have to start out all over again, relearning those familiar parts of ourselves that resist even the gentlest analysis and praying for a timely scepticism. As if as a child one had walked into a wet crumbling house and felt the tang of decay, emptiness, drab sky. The scar on her own white body ran like the shadow of a man's arm from beneath her child-fallen breasts to the small warmth of her loins. I'd look fine, she

107

thought as she comforted the child, on the inside pages of *Playboy* with my arms thrown open in tensed surprise like the cormorants we saw shading the waves from the island today. She threw open the window and pulled a deep orange robe over herself to get a drink downstairs for Eileen. The house was quiet. The boy in jeans and shirt was washing dishes in the kitchen and as he looked at her casually under his dark eyelids, she thought I'll take his mop of hair and squeeze his face between my legs so that he might scarcely breathe.

"I want to go home," said Eileen.

"Sleep now," the mother said and brushed Eileen's hair with her fingertips.

Judy walked through the sparse crowds, perhaps less euphoric now as they came into winter, their stale stomachs excruciated after the happy outrage of the long summer drinking, the headlights of a car brushing against the virginia creeper that nestled against the old university walls. She had hoped they might have driven out tonight to watch the wind spend itself on the drawn-grey stones of Connemara. Oh the myths the northerners love, the places where the troops will lie down! The chagrin burning on men's faces who expect answers that will confirm their own existence. In a small hostelry, up the dishevelled stairs among loud demurring students who flaunted an adopted Gaelic and what little knowledge of alcoholism they had, she drank pints of Guinness in the early flamboyant style of a girl celebrating new values and wisdom, eager for a person to steal a promise from the ennui of the drinkers. She interrupted conversations readily, her accent tending to be either American or from a corner of Kerry, unaware or scared of the laughter.

"Do you know that Will Byrne is a real old fountain-head?" she said, mimicking McFarland's accent.

"Belfast is the spiritual centre of Europe," she told a doctor.

"Fuck ye away from that house, ye bastards," old Byrne was shouting out of his lighted window and the dogs were barking, the duchess breaking away with raised hair through the long wet grass from the circling flames.

Meanwhile Furaisti and McFarland were rolling a stolen barrel of beer into a nurse's flat. The older man was out of breath and they had broken some strings on the fiddle. Four Connemara men in hats and coats stood drinking in the corridor with them, talking indifferently and happily among the endless traffic of people. They had a thirst like a chimney with a good draw. It took a while for McFarland to see confirmed in him and among the others a sense of other realities than being Irish, drink should let the mind wander to the present even foregoing the recent if not altogether past. And leaving in the dead of night, his arm round a friend, Saul spoke again. "Be like a fox boy, piss on your trail and scatter the drops to puzzle the scent." So McFarland to the air of the flogging reel took various routes home. And in the hotel the sound of his footsteps still came up the stairs to him, going from door to door searching for his room. Her clothes were scattered in a line to the bed. "I have never known a woman like her," he said as he lifted the sheets to Judy's chin and tucked her in next Eileen. He sat on the bed looking at them. In a word, Bach. Lord it is enough when it please Thee bring my life to a close, he placed the fiddle and bow on the chair. He read a few pages of Scott's travels, but his mind wandered to the time they alighted on Portaferry strand among the sunning ladies from the seagulls' clamour all night and all day, with a single seal dipping and spreading a long straight line on the ocean and how he thought that day his eyes might never focus again.

My trouble. In a word. Never lie on the left side, boy, you'll squeeze the heart out of yourself. Tom awoke and saw the match flare up in the dark and light up his father's face who had climbed awkwardly into bed beside him.

McFarland smoked in the darkness.

"Judy, Judy," he whispered across.

"Are you awake, Judy?"

"I heard tonight a story when Furaisti played 'Banish Misfortune'. It happened back in the days when death wasn't an institution. Jimmy Cummins turned to me and said, 'Do you hear that? Well, there was a piper from Gurteen, a fine piper in his day who drank nothing but French wine and oddly enough just played once in a fine house. He'd mind that night if he were alive today. For there the gentry's daughter came away with him, a lightsome girl and the parents naturally enough with acres of turnips and cabbages for setting disowned her. There was no hue or cry and the

Gurteen man took her on his short travels for money and baby clothes. For the girl was expecting a piper's baby and not long after she and the baby died in this town. The coffin was put up on a cart drawn by a dray horse and no one following from the cobbles of the Spanish Arch. And the piper began a lament, not too slow or too quick on account of his losses, and the men in the fever hospital sweating from their labours counted four thousand mourners as they crossed Loch Ataile for Forthill graveyard. That's banished misfortune for you,' said Jimmy Cummins."

"Do you hear me Judy?"

She heard him in a drunken vulgar way, accessible still for all his various frailties, but she was silent for in her heart of hearts she feared he was softening, losing his sense of justice, merely protesting that erratic comedy of life. Fear was so addictive, consuming all of a body's time and she wanted so much to share this vigil with him in Fermanagh but what could you give the young if they were barricaded from the present by our lyrical, stifling past? She said nothing, knowing she shared this empty ecstasy with a thousand others who had let their laziness go on too long.

"I left home too young, that's what bothers me," he spoke again. "There must be a thousand stories and songs about my own place that I hardly know. But when we return, woman, we'll try."

In a foot of land there's a square mile of learning, Saul had said, and he had learned to build from a sense of duty to the beauty of the hilly Erne.

For in April of 1910, Saul had a bad back but nevertheless he had finished building a church in Donegal town and now with Bimbo Flynn the whistler he set about kissing the air and erecting his own house. And it was a house where the best sessions of music would be held, where you could drive a tractor through the back windows. They gathered the red limestone rocks from the hills and fine washed stones from the Erne, the broached flagstones from Sliabh Buadh. Are you after work? he asked the grimy gypsies. God, you might swear mister, they said, and the gypsies carried cartloads of rocks up the hillside and sat under the chestnut tree smoking and drinking while it rained. His wife Olive came from the old house each day with tea and sandwiches for the men taking their time at their work on the edge of the woods that fell away to

the lake. He'll fire everything to get back to America, the neighbours said, knowing the long travelling of the McFarlands, but as
summer came he straightened up like a post in the good weather
and the roof edged across the sky.

"Let it pass by."

"Judy."

"Piss on them, boy, piss on them."

"Where are we for today then?"

"Men of Ireland."

"Do him no good to be a fife player now."

"I'd kill a man for that."

"Look, we'll hang the door tomorrow."

"Have done with it."

When the burning was a long time off they put in two rows of
slates as a damp course and timbered each room from the yellow
larch that crashed in a fine storm, Bimbo never tiring of the saw
that sang in his hands, his feet muffled in the knee-high sawdust
and the briars in the hair of the gypsy children. A bird nested in
the bodhran young Will Byrne, a great lad, had left in his father's
barn. Boys oh boys. And in July a stray Dalmatian came whistling
up through the grass to them of a Friday, his spots like squashed
blackberries, jumping round himself. They adopted him for the
new house. The iron shone on the range and the whistler fenced off
an orchard and set forty apple trees and Olive took great care
putting down their first rose bush. And folks wondered about the
ornamented porch that was built out front with the stained-glass
windows, and there was talk of a church but when the last stones
dried and you could hear the knock-knock of a thrush breaking a
snail in his new garden Saul was a proud man. Always before daylight a man thinks of his destiny, as Saul did that last morning
talking with the travellers in the half-light of the chestnut hill and
he was glad to see that the cream-coloured mare of the gypsies was
loath to leave the fine grass now that her time had come.